Ready To Wed

USA TODAY BESTSELLING AUTHOR

J.L. BERG

BY THE BAY SERIES

The Choices I've Made

The Scars I Bare

The Lies I've Told

The Mistakes I've Made

The Secrets We Keep

The Bridges I've Burned

By the Bay Series - The Box Set

STANDALONES

Fraud

The Tattered Gloves

The Affair

Chapter One

CLARE

"Where are my keys?" I shouted, running around the kitchen like a crazy person in search of my bright pink monogrammed key ring. It really shouldn't be that hard to miss.

"Why do you need keys?" asked Logan, my smug looking fiancé, as he casually leaned against the door frame.

"What do you mean? Aren't we leaving? Of course I need keys. Why are you just standing there? Start looking!" I commanded.

He didn't budge. He just continued his casual lean and grinned, looking cocky and gorgeous, before pulling his own set of keys out of his pocket.

"I don't really think we need both set of keys while we're away…do you?" he asked.

I just stared at him. Why was I so frantic and nervous? I'd spent the last twenty minutes looking for keys that I didn't need. I knew that. Logan was driving to the airport, so why did I need keys? Before the keys, I'd scrubbed down the entire kitchen from top to bottom after doing the same to all three bathrooms. Why? I have no freaking clue. Did I want the house to look nice just in case someone came to rob us? Because nothing says, "Welcome to our house, please take our television!" like clean bathrooms.

"You're right. I don't need my keys," I said calmly.

He left his post at the entryway and walked towards me, wrapping his arms around my waist. He pulled me closer to him and I sighed, settling into the warmth of his body instantly.

"Are you okay Clare? You've been wired ever since we started planning this a week ago. You know, we don't have to get married this weekend. We can postpone it. Like I've always said, I'll wait for you."

"No. I want to get married this weekend. It's just…there's a lot to do, and I feel like I'm going to forget something important," I answered.

"There are two things you need at that wedding," he said.

"Oh?"

"Mmmhmm….me and a ring. The rest is just for show."

"Don't forget me!" Maddie said, barreling into the kitchen from the hallway. My overly excited five year old couldn't wait to hop on that plane and go to "the beach". She didn't even care what beach, only that we were going and she got to play in the sand. The fact that Logan and I were getting married was the icing on the cake. God, I was lucky. I gave Logan a once over, checking for signs of weakness, symptoms that he might be tired or sick.

Well, mostly lucky.

"You got all of your new meds?" I asked, looking at Logan with concern.

"Yes, there are only a few for now."

"Are you sure….about waiting?"

Logan had just been diagnosed with Hodgkin's disease, and in an effort to not put our lives on hold, we decided to get married as soon as possible. His doctors were optimistic, saying that since it was caught early, his likelihood of recovery was high, but I still worried. My first husband, Maddie's father, had died of cancer. I still remember every single day, every minute watching helplessly as he deteriorated in front of me. I had been useless, completely useless, and unable to stop it.

"I'm sure. It's only a couple weeks. The oncologist said it would be okay to delay treatment for two weeks. I want to enjoy our wedding and time away with you. I'll start the minute we get home. I promise."

I nodded, giving him a hint of a smile before turning to Maddie.

"Are you ready?" I asked brightly.

"Yes, yes, yes!" she beamed.

"Well, let's go!"

We loaded the car and headed to the airport for our two week long stay in St. Thomas. It had originally been our vacation for the summer…the first trip Logan and I would take together. He was my first ray of hope since Ethan died. He showed me love can exist after death, even when it seems impossible. When he proposed, we turned our vacation into an impromptu wedding, renting out a small resort and inviting our family and few friends. Logan still wouldn't tell me how much everything cost. He just smiled and started whistling every time I asked. I had a feeling it was a crap load. I knew he could afford it, but it didn't make me feel less guilty.

"When do Leah and Garrett fly in?" Logan asked.

Leah was my best friend and Maid of Honor. She was flying in with my brother, who was a groomsman for Logan. Leah and Garrett loved each other like brother and sister and always tried to hang out whenever they could. My brother's crazy work schedule didn't offer him much time off, so they decided to book their tickets together to give them some time to catch up.

"Um, I think they come in a few hours after us. Leah had to work late last night, so she wanted to take a later flight. Garrett is supposed to be picking her up around noon."

"Do they...I mean, have Garrett and Leah ever...?" he asked, skirting around the question.

"Eww...gross! No!"

He lifted a hand from the steering wheel in mock defense, "Just asking...didn't want to make assumptions. I've only met your brother a handful of times. I don't think I've ever met anyone who works more than he does...and I'm a doctor."

"I know. My brother, the workaholic. Who knew he'd move back home from college and we'd still never see him," I said with a shrug.

After checking our luggage, including the very precious garment bag that contained my wedding dress, we went through security. This was always a fun task with a child, and we of course got several glaring looks from the speedy businessmen. Once securely checked, we proceeded to our gate.

"I can't believe they wouldn't let me carry on my garment bag!" I said with a huff.

"Well, it was quite large," Logan said, pointing to our gate and taking a seat in our designated area. Maddie immediately reached into the backpack of activities we'd packed, pulled out a book and began reading…or at least pretended. Either way she was being quiet, and I thanked the heavens for the few minutes of peace. I loved her more than I ever thought possible, but man…she could talk. I guess I shouldn't be surprised considering who gave birth to her. I'm not known for being quiet, especially when I'm nervous. I babble a lot.

"It wasn't that large! Okay…it was, but crap. They let that dude in front of us bring his guitar," I pouted.

"Hey," Logan said, pulling my chin level so our eyes were locked. "It will be fine. Nothing could ruin this week, okay? By the end of this weekend, you will be officially and forever mine. I don't care if you're in a burlap sack, Clare. The only thing that matters is that you say those vows and bind yourself to me for eternity, got it?"

"Yes," I said, a bit breathless.

"Good." He gave me a quick wink before pulling Maddie on his lap. She'd only learned a few words so far, so he assisted by helping her sound out the rest. I just watched, loving the perfect picture the two of them made. I would have never guessed, walking into that emergency room several months ago when

Maddie had fallen and given herself a concussion, that I would wind up here. Logan not only healed Maddie that day, he's been healing all of us ever since.

About thirty minutes later the announcement came that our flight was boarding, so we packed up Maddie's things and headed for the gate to check in. With Maddie bouncing up and down in his arms, Logan ran his free hand down my cheek, his eyes suddenly filled with emotion.

"Ready to go get married?" he asked.

"Absolutely."

Smiling, he grabbed my hand and we walked towards our future.

LOGAN

So many emotions hit me all at once when we boarded that plane to St. Thomas. The child in my arms was about to become my daughter. The woman I loved was about to become my wife.

A family. My family, finally.

It was something I'd always wanted, and here it was, all because I opened the right exam room door and found my future on the other side.

After a quick changeover in Charlotte, we were flying over water and headed for St. Thomas. Clare and Maddie had fallen asleep, both leaning their heads against my chest as I tried to read. I puffed out a small laugh and gave up, my awkward attempts at holding my e-reader with the two of them wedged against me proved fruitless. I tucked it in the front pocket of the seat in front of me, and rested my head against the seat, looking down at my two red-headed angels.

Maddie looked like a cherub plucked right out of heaven. Her strawberry blonde curls cascaded down her back in a fiery display, mimicking her mother's. Clare's red hair was deeper, more intense; closer to auburn but it still having that crimson glow to it that matched her personality. Sweet with just a touch of fire— that was my Clare. I never knew what I was going to get from one moment to the next, and that's what I loved about her. She kept me on my toes, loved me for who I was, and never let me be anything but myself.

I must have dozed off, because the next thing I knew I was being poked in the head by Maddie. *What did she have against my head?*

"You're awake!" she said brightly.

"Well, I am now, Princess!" I gave her side a pinch which caused her to giggle.

"Shhh! You'll wake up Mommy," I said, running my hand through Clare's hair as she rested against me. She really had been running around like mad the last week, so much so that I'd barely seen her. I knew planning the wedding start-to-finish inside one week had put a lot of pressure on her, so I tried not to take it personally. I just hoped that's all it was.

"So, Princess…what is the first thing you want to do when we get there?"

Figuring she'd say she wanted to go to the beach or swim in one of the many pools, her actual answer totally threw me for a loop.

"Ice cream. I want ice cream."

I silently laughed, being mindful of Clare.

"We fly all the way to St. Thomas and you want ice cream?" *Kids. Gotta love 'em.*

"Well, I've never been any other place but America. And ice cream is my favorite food. Is it different in different places?"

"Hmm…good point. I think we should check immediately, just to be sure."

She nodded, and I gave her a wink. She asked if she could watch a movie on the individual TV screens we had, and I said sure, letting her navigate the channels and pick her own movie. With one hand free now, I picked up my e-reader and started reading again, happy to have Clare warm and safe in my arms.

An entire kid's movie later, we were making our descent, and Maddie was plastered to the window looking out at the scenery below. It was quite the sight. Brilliant blue water contrasted with the deep green landscape. All I saw was my future. In a few days, on that island, I would marry Clare. I looked down at her as she began to stir and felt whole. Cancer or no…my life was perfect.

Chapter Two

CLARE

"Where is it?" I asked again, as we watched the endless luggage go around the noisy carousel in baggage claim. Maddie was doing circles around Logan's legs which he did an excellent job of ignoring. He was settling into his Dad role nicely, I laughed silently to myself.

"I'm sure it's coming," he answered, although I could see even he was starting to doubt his words.

All of our bags had come through the carousel… all but one. My garment bag. The one the stupid perky blonde lady at the counter had made me check. The garment bag she had assured me would be fine. Where the hell was it? How could I get married without a dress?

Just when I had created the ultimate list of ways in which I was going to let the customer service reps have it, my garment bag appeared, like a beacon from heaven.

"There it is! Oh thank God!" I squealed, running to the carousel like a manic child, only to be immediately halted when I saw the huge gash in the side. My once mint condition ivory dress was now spilling out of the hole in the side and ripped to shreds.

I heard Logan curse right before the tears started to sting my eyes. What the hell was I supposed to do now? Taking charge, Logan grabbed the garment bag off the carousel before it made another long journey around the airport, and held it up for inspection. Yep, it was a total loss unless we wanted to change things up and have a themed wedding; if I wanted to go as the Bride of Chuckie, I was golden.

"Do you think it's fixable?" he asked gently.

"No," I moaned, before covering my face with my hands.

"Oh no Mommy, your pretty dress is all messed up!"

Logan patted her on the head and said it was okay to give Mommy a hug. She happily came to my side, offering her sympathy in the form of child-sized hugs. They helped for about five seconds until

I saw that humongous gash again, and then the misery came rushing back.

Stupid airline. Stupid dress.

"I don't have a dress! What am I supposed to do without a dress? Do you think it's a sign? Maybe we aren't supposed to get married this week. Maybe this is one giant ivory colored sign that we are supposed to wait…go home, and get married later."

"Whoa…babe, you're babbling. Like, a lot." He gripped my shoulder and pulled me close. He smelled like aftershave and mint. Familiar and safe.

"Calm down. This is a wardrobe malfunction, not a cosmic sign from the universe, okay?"

I nodded, and pulled him closer, resting my head on his shoulder, knowing he was right. It was just the fact that with every step we took further away from home, away from that hospital and his doctors, I felt the panic growing and multiplying a bit more. I looked up at him and wondered, *Were we making the right choice in putting off his treatment?*

LOGAN

"Oh, thank fuck you're here!" I said, seeing Leah enter the hotel, with Garrett in tow.

"Well, it's nice to see you too, handsome," she answered with a wink and a sly grin. I helped them with their luggage and gave Garrett a friendly guy hug before turning back to Leah, my savior for the day.

"So, why are you so glad to see me? Not that I don't appreciate the welcome."

"Clare. She's freaking out. Her dress was trashed on the trip over here, and she is literally losing her shit. I don't know a thing about dresses. I don't have a clue on where to look, what she wants. And now she's got it in her head that this is some sort of sign that the entire wedding is doomed."

I started pacing the lobby because I really didn't know what else to do. I know weddings always had kinks, but ours was supposed to be low key. There were only a few guests, and yes…we threw it together in a few days and did it destination style, but still. Low key. *What happened to that?*

"Logan." I didn't answer, I just continued to pace, hoping an answer would magically appear to fix my freaked out bride.

"Logan, seriously. Look at me."

Leah sounded pretty damn serious, so I did as I was told and met her gaze. I'd learned to not mess with Leah. She could be kind of scary.

"Garrett, go take Logan out for drinks or something. I've got it from here."

"Wait, what?"

"You're dismissed. Didn't you hear me the first time?"

"Uh.."

"Go do dude stuff, and I will handle the distraught bride. I'm pretty sure I can find a wedding dress a lot faster than you can! We'll meet you for dinner!"

And just like that, Leah saved the day.

Chapter Three

"Okay, get up," Leah said, pulling my arm in a vain attempt to get my ass out of the lounge chair I was currently occupying.

"Nooo….I don't want to," I whined.

She looked at the little table next to my lounger and laughed.

"How many of those fruity cocktails have you had, Clare Bear?"

"Um…two, maybe?" I hiccuped a bit, and laughed. Okay, maybe a bit more than two.

"Was your plan to drink yourself a new wedding dress?"

I slumped back into my cozy lounge chair, enjoying the feel of the warm sun on my bare skin. After we arrived at the resort, a truly breathtaking place I might add, I dropped my ruined wedding dress in our suite and decided to take my sorrows poolside. The pool had sweeping, endless views of the ocean and the water seemed to disappear right into the blue horizon. Maddie was enjoying the kid's day program the resort offered, and I figured putting on my bikini and ordering a few drinks might improve my sour mood.

At least I was giggling and my mood felt a bit lighter. That was an improvement.

"No, but what am I supposed to do, Leah? Do you see a wedding shop here?" I asked, sweeping my hands in a grand gesture to point out the obvious. We were in paradise. There were bars, restaurants and tourist traps, but definitely no places to buy a wedding gown. I was screwed. Maybe I should just get married in that burlap sack Logan mentioned… or a bikini. He'd definitely like that a lot more than a sack.

"What are you grinning about?"

"What? Nothing."

"Shit, you're totally tossed."

"Am not."

"Are too."

"Nah uh," I argued, but the words slurred and totally ruined my argument. I laughed.

"Oh, for fuck's sake, Clare!" she said, trying not to grin. I could see she was trying to be serious, but she was doing a terrible job of it because the corners of her mouth were struggling to stay turned down and she finally had to turn away.

"Come on, Leah! Have a drink with me! My wedding is ruined…let's get drunk! Well, I mean I'm already there…so you just need to catch up!"

She whipped her head around and planted her sundress clad body on the lounger next to mine. Her blonde hair and sun kissed legs looked right at home in this tropical location. I, on the other hand, with my freckled pale skin and red hair, looked like I hopped on the wrong plane. The only way I could stand the sun was slathering on four layers of sunscreen and wearing a huge floppy hat.

"You two are going to drive me insane by the end of the week. Listen to me, your wedding is not ruined. You had a setback, that's it. We are going to get a driver and I'm going to talk to the concierge and we are going to find you a dress, come hell or high water. Got it?"

Snorting and trying to mask my laughter, I nodded; Bossy Leah always cracked me up. I loved her to death and she always managed to take charge when needed, but when she took on her alter ego and started barking orders and taking charge, I couldn't help but grin. It reminded me of the little girl who stood up for me in that cafeteria so many years ago and instantly became my lifelong best friend.

"So, get your cute ass upstairs, change, and meet me in the lobby in fifteen minutes!"

"Yes, Ma'am!"

"And I'll get you some coffee."

"I like sugar!" I sung, as I started for the sliding door back into the hotel.

"Mmmhmm…I know. And for fuck's sakes, wrap a towel around that shit before your fiancé has to kill half the crew for hitting on you."

"Oh," I laughed. "Oops."

I grabbed a towel from the stack next to the door, and wrapped it around my scantily clad body. The last thing I saw was Leah shaking her head and laughing as I haphazardly made my way back to my hotel room.

"Drink it all," Leah said, shoving a huge cup of coffee in my hand as I walked out of the elevator fifteen minutes later. Dressed in jean shorts and a green tank top, I was ready for whatever adventure she'd mapped out for us. I tried to have faith, but I was really doubting that I'd be able to find a new dress with such limited time before the big day. I'd barely been able to find the first dress, having just enough time to visit two stores in a single afternoon. The dress I'd bought was off the rack, of course, and one of the few in my size. It was beautiful, well…not anymore.

"Yes, Ma'am!" I said again, snickering.

"Mommy is funny today!"

"Yep, sure is," Leah said, giving me a wry look.

While I was upstairs changing, Leah had picked up Maddie from the day camp and asked if she wanted to help us shop. Being the little diva she was, she naturally agreed.

"Let's go shopping, ladies!" Leah said cheerfully, and all of us, including my extra-large cup of coffee with cream and sugar, headed out of the hotel and into the black rented sedan Leah had managed to obtain.

"The concierge gave me a couple places to check out, but based on everything she told me, there is one place I want to go to first."

I gave her a thumbs up and we were on our way.

"I think you should get a pink dress Mommy."

"Oh yeah? I'm not sure pink is my color baby girl."

She gave me a pointed look that could only be pulled off by a five year old and said, "Pink is every-one's color Mommy."

Put in my place by my own offspring. *Figures.*

"Well, if there is a pink dress…I promise I'll try it

on." I gave Leah a wink, knowing full well I wouldn't have to keep my word. What kind of bridal shop had pink dresses?

I really should have kept my mouth shut, because as soon as we walked into the door of the beautifully decorated bridal salon Leah had chosen, in all its pink, glittery glory, was a dress that would have put Glenda the Good Witch to shame.

I think I almost went deaf from the squeals that emanated from my daughter.

"Mommy! You have to try this on!"

At least she said I just had to try it on. Based on the decibel level of that squeal, I figured she would have demanded I buy it on the spot.

No doubt hearing the noise from our grand entrance, a store clerk emerged and gave us a warm welcome. She was the nicest woman you could ask for when shopping for a wedding dress. A complete contrast to the stores I visited back home. They were all rush, rush…and highly annoyed I had come in at the last minute. Who gets married that quickly? *Um, lots of people.* Get over it. And no, I wasn't pregnant. But thanks for giving me the once over.

Was it a crime that I wanted to look good on my special day, even if it wasn't a year in the future?

The woman helping us, Maria, seemed to understand perfectly, having most likely helped plenty of women in similar situations. We weren't in Vegas, but with views and romance surrounding you at every turn in this place, impromptu weddings were likely to occur.

"What type of dress were you looking for?" she asked, which took me by surprise.

"Whatever you have off the rack, I guess."

"Oh darling…we have plenty. Tell me what you envision wearing the day you marry your special man, and I will see what I can do."

Maybe it was the alcohol, maybe I was overly emotional from everything that was happening…but I began to tear up. Leah threw an arm around me and gave me a gentle hug.

"See, I told you we would find you something special. Did you ever stop to think that maybe your dress getting trashed wasn't a sign that you weren't supposed to get married, but a sign that you weren't supposed to get married in that dress?"

I looked up at her confused.

"Clare, don't try and hide it. I know you hated that dress."

I tried to argue with her, but I couldn't. I really did hate that dress. It was, like I said, beautiful…with a sweeping matte satin train and fitted strapless bodice…but it wasn't me at all.

"When I see myself on that beach, marrying Logan, I see myself in vintage lace. Something simple— timeless and elegant, but not overdone."

Maria smiled, "I think I have just the thing."

LOGAN

"She's going to kill you, man," my soon to be brother in law said, shaking his head as I moved the last bag across the hall.

"I might kill myself first."

"They're not back yet. You could still change your mind. She'd never know."

I stopped in the middle of the hall, looking back and forth between the two doors and shook my head.

"No, I want to do this. I think we need a bit of tradition."

"Okay, but do me one favor?"

"Sure, what's that?"

"Let me be around when you tell her?" he said, before hitting me on the back and laughing. I groaned, hating myself already.

We didn't have to wait long. After finishing the task that would no doubt land me in the dog house, we headed downstairs to the bar and met the girls in the lobby, returning from their afternoon out. My eyes came to rest on Clare, and I felt my breath hitch. Even after months together, waking up each morning by her side, day after day, she still managed to steal my breath with just one glimpse.

She was glowing, full of joy, and no longer carrying that devastated expression she'd arrived with after finding her destroyed wedding dress.

Instantly, I was at her side. Bending down, I placed a lingering, tender kiss on her lips.

"I'm guessing it was a good trip?"

She smiled against my lips, and nodded.

"Leah, could you take Maddie to the pool for an hour or so, while I unpack with Logan?"

Her eyes had that look. That mischievous, want-to-fuck-you look. I was so screwed.

"Yep. On it. Come on, Short Stack!"

Leah picked up a giggling Maddie and headed upstairs to Leah's room to change. Maddie, deciding that since she was at the beach, a swim suit must be worn at all times. She was hopping up and down, ready to jump in. Leah kept tickling her, telling her to be patient. Garrett looked back at us, obviously trying to decide whether or not he wanted to be around for my bomb drop, and finally gave us a salute and hurried after Leah, catching her in the elevator just before it closed.

It was just her and me. She looked up with those seductive green eyes I adored and pulled my hand towards the elevator.

"So, about upstairs…," I started, but was interrupted the second the elevator doors closed. Clare pushed me against the wall with her free hand, holding her garment bag with the other and pressing her body against mine. She teased me with a light kiss, nipping at my bottom lip with her teeth, before taking charge in an all-consuming kiss that left me dizzy.

My brain went haywire, and I lost the ability to think beyond her and how good her lips felt, how I wanted to take her right there in that elevator and if she didn't stop kissing me like that, I would.

I don't remember how, but somehow we made it out of the elevator when it came to our floor and to our suite. I swiped the keycard and we all but fell into the room. Immediately after closing the door, I had her pinned to it, running my hands down the curve of her ass to hook her legs around me. She wrapped both of her arms around my neck. I had no idea where the garment bag went and at that point I didn't fucking care. I said she could get married in a burlap sack, and I meant it.

Pinned securely to the wall, her hand went to the front of my shorts, palming my hard length through the fabric. Just that one touch from her could end me. God, what the hell was I thinking earlier? I needed to go across the hall and move everything back before she noticed.

Her eyes focused on me, a pleased smile spreading across her face, knowing she could bring so much pleasure with such a small gesture.

Just as I was about to reciprocate, dive my hand into the juncture of her thighs and feel that wet heat I loved, her eyes moved away from mine and focused on the room.

"Where are the rest of the suitcases?"

Fuck.

"Uhhh…"

"Logan, where are your suitcases?"

"Across the hall?" I don't know why I phrased it like a question. Like that would help.

"Across the hall? Why?"

"It doesn't matter. Forget it. I'll move them back." I moved in to kiss her, wanting to get back to the naughty fun we were having, but she turned her head, giving me an amused and slightly pissed look.

"*You* moved them? Why would you do that?"

I ran my hands up her shirt, still intent on distracting her. She slapped away my hand. I was not getting out of this.

"I thought it might be nice for the two of us to… you know, not be together until the wedding. A bit of tradition."

"Oh, I see."

Well, that wasn't so bad.

"And what is this exactly?" she asked, referring to the fact that I had her pressed against the door of our once shared suite, seconds away from stripping her naked and fucking her until she screamed my name so loud all the neighbors heard.

"I decided, after a bit of thinking, that it was a dumb idea…so I'm moving everything back."

She gave me a mischievous grin. A very different type of mischief though than what I witnessed in the lobby. Whatever she was thinking now, I had a feeling I wouldn't be enjoying it.

"No I think it's a great idea," she said, sliding her beautiful legs down to the ground, and giving my body a slight push off hers.

"You do?"

"Oh yeah. What is that saying? Distance makes the heart grow fonder?"

She sauntered away, bending down to pick up the garment bag she'd dropped in our mangled entrance minutes ago. She made a show of it too, sticking her ass up and bending down slowly.

How many days until we got married? Three?

I was so fucked.

Chapter Four

CLARE

"Men are so dumb," Leah laughed, having just heard about my afternoon nookie that wasn't.

"I know! So, now, I'm holding him to it. If he thought it was such a great idea, then we'll do it. Separate rooms and no sex until our wedding night."

"That's mean," she said.

"Oh, no. What's mean is that I'm going to make it hell for him." I emphasized my point, perking up my boobs that were on full display in my very revealing teal dress I'd chosen for dinner.

"Okay, now that's just evil. Good job." She gave me a high five.

We continued to laugh and enjoy our relaxed time together. We didn't have a lot of it back home.

One of us usually had to run off and we never had enough time. She worked full time as a nurse, and I had Maddie and now Logan. Our lives were chaotic, but we always made time for each other.

After an hour or so, everyone else joined us for dinner. We had a large party. My parents had flown in just a few hours ago, along with Logan's best friend Colin and his wife Ella who brought along their newborn son. We all ooh'ed and ahh'd over Colin's mini-me before settling down to eat. Maddie had spent the afternoon swimming with Leah, and when my parents arrived, she took them on a tour of the grounds, showing them where all of her favorite spots were. She'd only been here for a few hours longer than them, but she was the expert. Naturally.

Logan sat down next to me, noticing my dress right away. His eyes widened and zeroed in on the cleavage billowing out. This was going to be fun.

"Nana, did you know that ice cream tastes even better on an island?" Maddie said to my mother, who had just taken her seat next to my father. Both were dressed casually and looked happy and relaxed. I was so glad to have them here.

"I didn't know that! You'll have to show me!"

"Logan took me right when we got off the plane and he got chocolate and I got mango. It was yummy!"

"So yummy, she got it all over her dress," Logan

exclaimed, giving her a nudge which made her giggle.

Kids can never eat ice cream without making a royal mess. It's like they don't understand the concept of how to lick the ice cream. Only mash. *Lick the ice cream? Okay Mommy!* Five seconds later, the kid is covered in it from head to toe.

"You forgot to mention that I got chocolate, but I didn't actually get to eat any of it," Logan said, giving me a look.

"Your fault. You shouldn't have ordered chocolate. You should know better by now."

"I asked you if you wanted any and you said no!"

"Still your fault."

I love chocolate. A lot. Bordering on slightly obsessed? Maybe. He should know not to bring any around me. I've been stealing chocolate and desserts from him since our first date. Even before, actually.

All throughout dinner, I caught Logan staring at me. He was distracted and would have to be asked questions more than once before he could answer. My teal man-killing dress was working.

Was making my fiancé miserable days before our wedding mean? Maybe. But it was fun.

That dress. That god damn dress. Where the hell did she get it? And how soon could I peel it off of her? I knew what she was doing. I knew she was playing me...pushing all my buttons to punish me for moving out of our suite.

Men are dumb. We make stupid mistakes. A lot.

Even the smartest of us, no matter how many Ivy League degrees we may have nailed to our walls, are stupid as fuck when it comes to the opposite sex. I realized this about half a second too late—right around the time I had my fiancée pinned against a door, ready to devour her.

Tradition? A little time apart? *Fuck that.* I tried to move back in immediately, but no...the damage had already been done.

Clare had already initiated my punishment before I had formed the words of my apology. And now that punishment was right up in my face—two round perfect breasts surrounded by a teal dress that was probably illegal in some countries. She leaned forward laughing, and I got an even better view down that valley of sin.

Dying. I was dying.

Shifting slightly, hoping to not draw attention to my now very uncomfortable position, I tried to get back into the conversation that was taking place at the table. But all I could see was Clare; her dark red hair, creamy smooth skin, and emerald green eyes that had held me prisoner since the moment I met her. A very willing prisoner, mind you. I had no plans of ever escaping.

She was my world. She had given me everything I'd ever wanted in life. If someone had asked the old me whether I thought one person could bring such happiness to your life, I would have laughed in their face. I'd spent a lifetime being screwed over by those who were supposed to love me, and finally when I found someone to love me back, I couldn't return those feelings. I'd decided love was something that was taught, learned from an early age and since my upbringing was less than warm and fuzzy, I'd missed out on those essential lessons needed to love another.

Meeting Clare had taught me otherwise. Her very presence showed me that I was so much more. Love was more than just a lesson or an acquired skill, and in a few days, she would be my wife. Mine to love and cherish forever.

She laughed again, the musical melody of her laugh bringing a smile to my face even though I had no idea what was being said. She lit up my entire world.

Clare's parents rose from their seats, thanking everyone for dinner and headed to bed. Apparently dinner was over. How long had I spaced out? Everyone else said their goodnight, and Clare, Maddie, and I headed upstairs to our suites. Plural.

God, I really was an ass.

"What's an ass?" Maddie asked as we exited the elevator on the top floor.

I looked at her, and quickly to Clare who was giving me a death stare. A slightly amused one, but a death stare nonetheless.

Great, I was thinking out loud now. Is this what happens when I went too long without touching Clare? *Would I go crazy?*

"Uhh…I said pass. Yeah, pass. I was thinking that we needed to get season passes for the amusement park when we got home."

"The season is just about to end," Clare said, arching her brow, almost as if she were challenging me.

"Well, for next year then. Never hurts to plan ahead, right?"

Maddie then launched into a ten minute conversation about what rides were her favorite and what order she would ride them and how much she loved cotton candy, especially the pink kind because pink was her favorite color. By the time we got her calmed down, she was dressed for bed and cuddling her favorite stuffed animal. We said goodnight and softly shut the door behind us.

It took about five seconds for Clare to burst out laughing.

"Season passes?"

"It was the only thing I could think of!" I said defensively. "Besides, I didn't hear you offering anything up."

"What were you muttering about anyway?" she asked, still snickering about my less than PG mumbling.

"I don't even remember. No sex is driving me bat shit crazy, Clare! You must take pity on me…for both of our sakes. Otherwise, I could be clinically insane by the time we take our vows, and then how would you know I actually mean them?"

"You're seriously asking for a pity lay?"

I sauntered over to her, grabbed her around the waist and pulled her body to mine with a bit of force, causing her to gasp in surprise. I let my lips hover over hers.

"I can assure you, a lay with me will never be pitiful."

I think her brain went offline for a moment or two, because her eyes glazed over and she licked her lips hungrily, causing me to groan. I bent down to finally take her perfect red lips, only to be stopped with a single finger. I guess her brain came back online. *Damn.*

"I think you have a room to go to," she said, her

finger still holding court on my deprived lips. Her mouth was upturned in a slight smile, but her eyes still looked a bit unfocused, like she was fighting the desire as much as I was. Good, at least I knew this was affecting her as much as me.

I sighed, knowing she'd won the battle tonight, but only tonight. There was always tomorrow. We were going snorkeling, and she could never resist a shirtless Logan. The thought brought a smirk to my face as I turned and made my exit.

"Well, just in case you get lonely or cold…you know where to find me!" I said, before giving her one last panty dropping smile and exiting the room.

Clare – one, Logan – zero. That would have to change tomorrow.

Chapter Five

CLARE

I'd never been snorkeling, but lounging outside on the sun-drenched beach next to my sexy as sin fiancé wasn't a bad way to spend an afternoon. I was becoming mesmerized by the way his dark blue swim trunks hung low on his hips. I could just make out the beginning of that "V" I so loved to trace with my tongue when we were alone. I licked my lips just thinking about it.

His hair was messy and yet completely put together. I have no idea how guys did that. I know, from living with him, he did little with it. He just ran his hands through it and *poof!* Magic hair! Me, on the other hand? When I woke up, it looked like a small woodland creature had taken residence in my red locks overnight. I had a thing for Logan's hair. It was one of the first things I noticed about him when we met, his gorgeous, just-fucked hair. And now, I knew from experience…it looked even better after a good roll in the sheets.

"You're staring at me," Logan said, his eyes still closed as he soaked up the sun.

"Well, there's a lot to stare at," I answered back.

"Well, anytime you want to transition from staring to touching, just let me know."

The corner of his mouth turned up into a half smirk, and I couldn't help but laugh. He was relentless. My little game of revenge had turned into an all-out war. Which one of us would cave first? I'd won round one last night, but then he showed up at my door this morning in a towel, water dripping off his perfect hair, running down his shoulders and broad chest, and I forgot how to speak. I stood there, momentarily stunned for God only knows how long, until I heard him say, "Hey, did you hear what I said?" Uh, no…how could I concentrate on anything else but those tiny beads of water dripping down his body?

He chuckled, "I said, do you have any toothpaste? I'm out."

I took one last look at up and down his scrumptious body, trying not to whimper as I walked away to retrieve the requested item. I almost caved, almost gave in right then and there. Had it not been for

Maddie barreling out of her room asking for breakfast, I probably would have pulled him by the towel into the room and tackled him to the ground.

The shower trick was low. He knew how much I loved him in a towel. It reminded me of our first morning together. We'd woken up and showered together, and I finally felt like I had found home again.

Before I had a chance to come up with a witty comeback to his touching comment, our instructor showed up; he was a tanned young surfer dude with blonde hair and an accent to match his laid back style. We both stood to greet him, and he kindly shook our hands, but his eyes lingered on me, and Logan noticed.

"Nice to meet you, Derek. I'm Logan, and this is my *fiancée,* Clare. We're here for the week celebrating our upcoming wedding." It wasn't lost on me that he emphasized the word fiancée or immediately wrapped a possessive arm around my waist.

"Well, it's nice to meet you both. Very nice," he said, his eyes still trying to lock with mine. Not happening, dude.

"Well, who's ready to get wet?!" he said with enthusiasm. Logan's hand gripped my hip harder and I sighed.

Oh, this was going to be fun.

. . .

I hated snorkeling. If that guy looked at Clare one more time, I swore I was going to shove his air tube up his ass. Note to self, request old, gay instructor next time.

"Okay, guys…had a great time. Thanks for spending the afternoon with me," the douche said, before he narrowed in on Clare. "If you need any one-on-one time in the future, please be sure to ask for Derek."

Clare's eyes widened a bit before giving a polite nod. She said thank you, which was more politeness than I could offer up at the moment. It was all I could do to keep my mouth shut. It takes a special kind of asshole to flirt with your fiancée right in front of you days before your wedding. The asshole in question sauntered away, no doubt thinking Clare was checking him out as he did. She wasn't. She had turned to me, her eyes full of laughter.

"You're jealous. And mad."

"That was not fun."

"You're kind of hot when you're mad," she said, rising up on her tip toes to place a soft kiss on my mouth. Not giving her the chance to move away, I pulled her closer, deepening the kiss as I moved my tongue with hers. She moaned, making that sound I loved, and melted in my arms. I needed to pull away and stop before the semi I was now sporting went pro. Covering up a boner in swimming trunks was nearly impossible, and there was no way I was going to do so out in the open with our relatives and friends milling about.

I reluctantly pulled back, running my fingers down the side of her face, into her damp hair. The sun was hot, and her hair had already started to dry in waves against her back.

"Giving up so easily, Mr. Matthews?" she teased.

"Just trying to keep my sanity, Mrs. Matthews-to-be. If I keep going, I won't be able to stop, and then your family will end up getting quite the show."

She snorted out a laugh, giving me a playful slap on the chest.

"Come on, Casanova, let's go find Maddie. I think her day program will be wrapping up soon and I wanted to take her shopping."

I bent down to pick up our stuff which was still resting near the lounge chairs we had occupied earlier. As soon as I came back up, the world tilted, and my vision blurred. I grabbed the first thing I could find, the lounger, but I missed, or I think I did. All I know was I ended up on the sand, with the lounge chair upended next to me.

"Oh my God! Logan! Logan! Are you okay?"

Clare came rushing to my side, kneeling down to pull me into her lap. I was dizzy, so dizzy. I looked around, my vision returning back to normal a bit, but still a bit fuzzy. Clare's father and mother were rushing over to us.

"I'm fine. I'm okay," I said, trying to rise. "I just need some water."

She dove into her beach bag, retrieving a bottle of water, and handed it to me. I took a few sips and let the water slid down my throat.

"Mom, go to the hotel. Have the front desk get a car ready. We need to get him to the hospital."

"No," I said simply.

"What?" Clare looked at me suddenly, her eyes filled with horror.

"Babe, I'm fine. Just a bit of dizziness. It's passing."

"But, what if…"

"Laura, Tom…can you give us a minute?" I asked Clare's parents. They nodded, both still looking at me with concern. I understood. Everyone here had already lost someone to cancer. But I wasn't going anywhere, and they needed to stop walking on egg shells.

After Laura and Tom walked back to their spot on the beach, not too far away, I looked up at Clare. Her eyes brimmed with tears, and she looked half a second away from sobs.

"Babe, come here," I said softly, opening my arms so she could fill them. She came willingly like she always did. We sat in the sand, holding each other for a minute while I gathered my thoughts. She pulled back finally, meeting my gaze, waiting for answers.

I took another sip of water, trying to keep the dizziness at bay. "This has nothing to do with the cancer, okay? Remember, I have no symptoms yet. They caught it early."

"Then why did I just watch you almost pass out a minute ago?"

"It's the meds they put me on. That, combined with the heat. I haven't had enough to drink, so I got dehydrated. I should have been watching my fluids. I'm a damn doctor, you would think I'd know this… but we're usually the worst patients."

"Well, then why the hell are we still outside!" she demanded, immediately jumping to her feet and trying to pull me with her. I weighed a good deal more than her so it was like trying to lift a bear. I helped her, rising to my feet slowly so that I wouldn't get dizzy again.

We made our way inside, where she continued to fuss over me for the rest of the afternoon. After more water and a bit of food, I was back to normal, but I feared Clare was anything but.

Chapter Six

LOGAN

After a mid-afternoon nap, I was feeling like my old self again. The dizziness was completely gone, and I wanted nothing more than to find my gorgeous fiancée and spent the rest of the evening with her wrapped in my arms.

I knew she was supposed to be pool side with Leah and Maddie, so I threw on some board shorts, ran my hands through my hair and hurried out to the door in search of my family. I just about took out Leah in my attempt.

"Oh my God, Logan, would you slow down?" Leah said, catching her breath after having probably lost a year or two of her life from being scared out of her mind when I came barreling out of my hotel suite straight into her.

"Sorry! Was just in a hurry to get to…hey, aren't you supposed to be down at the pool with Clare and Maddie?" I asked suspiciously. I could see the straps of her bathing suit peeking out from under her cover up and a towel was tucked under her arm, but there was no Maddie or Clare anywhere.

"I was, but they never showed. I was on my way to investigate. Want to help?" she asked with an arched brow.

My answer was to turn and knock on Clare's door. It wasn't like her to blow off Leah without so much as a word. I know it was only a trip to the pool, but Clare was raised in the South and her manners were impeccable. I took her to a dinner party a week or so ago, not really explaining where we were going, and she about died when we showed up…without a hostess gift. A hostess gift? What the hell was that? Apparently it was a thing; a big thing to Clare. The next day she'd sent a card and a gift to apologize for her fiancé's oversight. Living in the South was a new and different world.

After a few moments, the door finally opened and Clare emerged, dressed in a pair of yoga pants and tank top. Definitely not pool attire.

"Oh. Hey, guys," she said, before turning around and walking back into the bedroom. Leah and I turned to each other confused, before walking into the suite together.

I looked around and everything was as neat as a pin. There were no clothes, no shoes…nothing. It looked like it did the first moment we walked in a few days ago. *What the hell was going on?*

Before I had a second longer to ponder, I heard soft sobs coming from Maddie's room. I immediately went to her, opening the bedroom door to find her curled up on her bed with her knees tucked under her chin. She was dressed in her hot pink Dora the Explorer bathing suit and a towel was lying next to her.

"Hey, Princess. What's the matter?"

Her eyes opened and focused on me and she briefly wiped away the tears before sitting up. I sat down next to her and she curled her body into mine. I loved when she did this. It was natural now. She didn't even have to think about it. When I put her to bed, or snuggled with her on the couch, she just melted into me. Such trust. I didn't know how in the world I ever deserved it, but I would spend the rest of my life trying to be a man who was worthy of it.

"Mommy says we have to go home."

My stomach fell to the floor and I couldn't breathe.

"What?" I managed to say, before looking up to see Leah's horrified face. She had stopped at the entry way, obviously not wanting to overwhelm

Maddie…but still curious as to what had made our girl cry.

"I told her I didn't want to leave the beach. I told her I wanted to see her in her pretty dress."

"And what did she say?" I asked hesitantly.

"She said I would, but not yet. She said we had to get home. It wasn't safe staying here."

I took a deep breath. Clare was freaking out again. She was panicking and rushing home where she felt safe. Where she felt I was safe.

"It's okay Princess. We're not going anywhere okay? I'll fix it."

"Are you sure? Mommy said…"

"I know what she said, but I'll change her mind, okay?"

"Okay."

"Leah, can you take Maddie to the pool for a bit while I talk to Clare?"

"Sure thing!" she said brightly, trying to lighten the mood. "Come on, Short Stack," she said, holding out her hand to Maddie, "Let's go play in the water!"

Maddie held her hand out to Leah and gave a small giggle which was progress. Leah scooped her up and exited the bedroom. By the time they were leaving the suite, I could hear the two laughing. One girl down, one more to go.

There were times during Ethan's illness when I liter-ally thought my chest was caving in. The doctors told me it was due to stress. Acute panic attacks, I guess. Sometimes there were just too many things to remember—what drugs he was supposed to take and when, what doctor's appointments to go to on what days, and what needed to be done…just in case. I kept my cool most of the time. I kept my brave face to show Ethan and the rest of the world. But there were times when I literally couldn't breathe…when it felt like there were so many thoughts in my head that if I had just one more, it would literally explode.

And that's when I would just shut down. I think it was for my own sanity. An off switch or some-thing would engage and I would just shut down for a few hours until the breath returned to my lungs and my chest felt like it was back to its normal size.

As I was packing everything back into my suit-case the day before my wedding, I wondered how quickly we could get a flight back to Richmond. Listening to my daughter cry in the room next to me, I felt like I was moments away from that switch being flipped again.

He passed out. Right in front of me. The doctors told us he was going to be fine. We caught it early they said. A little bit of chemo and radiation and it should be fine, they said. I took a breath and stopped worrying after they told us that. He wasn't Ethan. There wasn't anything poisoning his brain, and he wasn't going to die on me. We would get through this. Right after we said our vows and celebrated our marriage.

But then he nearly passed out on that beach and I forgot how to breathe again. Every fear, every moment of agony came rushing back. I told myself I would fight for him…that I would be strong for us. But…Oh God, what if the doctors were wrong? What if he wasn't okay? What if he died, just like Ethan and I became a widow…again.

Neat folding turned into frantic packing. I started tossing everything in the suitcase without any sort of organization. TSA would just screw it all up right? I took one last look at my wedding dress, tucked away in its garment bag and put those sad thoughts behind me.

We needed to go home. Logan needed to go home. I would not lose another husband.

A knock on the door pulled my attention from thoughts and I saw Logan come into the bedroom. I had completely forgotten I had let him and Leah in a few minutes ago. I was so lost in myself I had barely registered opening the door.

"Hey, what is this I hear about us leaving?" he

said, walking forward to take a seat on the bed next to me.

"We need to go home. I don't feel right being here. You need to be home, with your doctors and immediate care if you need it."

"And our wedding?" he asked.

I physically flinched at the reminder. By this time tomorrow, had things been different, Leah and my mother would be helping me into my wedding gown, making the final touches to my makeup. We would most likely be laughing as we watched Maddie twirl around in her dress, elated over her role as flower girl.

"We can wait. I just…I need you to be okay."

I looked up just then into the eyes of the man I'd fallen in love with; the man who had stolen my heart, and saw nothing but love. His steel gray eyes held mine and I could do nothing but stare back into their depths.

Without breaking eye contact, he took my hand in his, intertwining our fingers and bringing them to his heart.

"Do you feel that?"

I nodded, feeling the warm, solid beat of his heart below my fingertips.

"That's me telling you I'm right here, and I'm going to be right here forever, babe. I know you're scared. I know you're trying to be brave, but please don't run."

"I'm not running."

"Yes, you are. You're running back to where you feel safe. Whisking me back to my doctor, taking me to the hospital isn't going to change anything. We were just there. I passed out because I had a bit too much sun. Let it be that, okay? But please, stay here with me. Marry me tomorrow. Become my wife. Because nothing is going to make me stronger than having you by my side."

Before another second passed, I leaned forward, fusing my body to his and kissing him like it was my last dying wish. He instantly responded, flipping me so my back was flat against the mattress, as he hovered above me.

"Don't tease me, Clare," he warned. His eyes were already darker, and I could feel how much he wanted me. He gently rocked into the apex of my thighs just to remind me how hard and ready I'd made him.

"I'm not teasing."

That's all it took. He was on me in nanoseconds. His hands were everywhere, running up the inside of my thighs, pushing up my tank top to rip my bra from my body.

"Don't ever make me wait that long again," he said taking my breast in his hand, gently flicking the nipple with his thumb causing my toes to curl. "I think I almost went crazy."

"Oh God, yes," I moaned as his head descended on my breast, taking my taut peak into his mouth.

"Good, we agree. No sex is bad."

For the next several hours, he continued to remind me exactly how much I missed over the last few days.

Chapter Seven

LOGAN

The elevator door closed with a soft click, and I turned to my beautiful bride to be. The moment our eyes collided, she lost her cool and burst into a fit of laughter.

"It's thirty minutes after seven," she said, trying to cover her laughter with her hand. Her vintage engagement ring twinkled under the bright lights above.

"Uh huh," I confirmed.

"We're late for our own rehearsal."

I smirked, remembering twenty minutes earlier when a very happy and contented Clare was sprawled out on our bed. She'd been naked and sighing peacefully from the three orgasms she'd just screamed out under my expert touch. She stretched like a cat, looked over at the clock and froze.

"Oh shit!" she'd said. "We're going to be late!"

"Late for what?" I'd said, crawling up her body, more than ready for round two…or three. I'd lost count.

"Our rehearsal! We're getting married tomorrow!"

"Oh shit!" We'd both shouted in unison, as clothes went flying and buttons were snapped and hair was tamed.

We flew out of our hotel suite and made it to the elevator in record time. And now we couldn't hold in the laughter. We were late to our own rehearsal because we'd been too busy…getting busy upstairs.

"Oh God, I'm never going to be able to look your father in the eye again," I said.

"Oh my God, you don't think he'll know, do you?" she asked, completely mortified.

"Have you taken a look at us Clare? Your clothes look like they were thrown on while sharing a car with a bunch of clowns, and my hair? You can actually see Clare sized dents in it from where you were holding on for dear life."

She turned and took a good look in the floor to ceiling mirror of the elevator. Her eyes went wide as she took in her appearance. I thought she looked fucking hot, but I knew the exact reason she looked that way. She looked thoroughly used, and really damn happy about it. But I didn't exactly like the idea of my future father in law seeing her that way.

She started to quickly adjust her skirt and tank top, making it look more presentable. She grabbed her large mane of burgundy red hair and tied it in a bun at the nape of her neck. Within seconds, she went from sexy vixen to classy woman, and I loved both.

The elevator dinged, and as we exited, she gave me a knowing smile. Then she glanced up and suddenly looked horrified, "Fix your hair!" she whispered.

I laughed, but did as I was told, trying to smooth down my dark tresses without much luck. She always told me I had "just fucked" hair so I didn't know exactly what she wanted me to do with it. I ran my hands through it, and messed it up a bit and she seemed pleased.

As we walked outside to our ceremony site, we were greeted by just about everyone we knew.

"They're here!" Leah yelled, "Finally!" She gave us a look. One that said she knew exactly why we were late.

We were then rushed around and put in places and everything that happened after that was a blur. I always thought rehearsals were strange. It was like dry humping; Almost, but not the real thing. There was a nice dinner afterwards, and toasts were delivered, but no one actually got married and I definitely didn't get a wedding night. We were spending the night apart...Our wedding party had made sure of that.

Well, at least I'd taken care of us ahead of time.

"Why are you grinning like a moron?" Leah asked, smacking the back of my head.

"Just so damn happy," I shrugged.

"Gonna go puke now," she muttered, as we all made our way to the restaurant, having finished our practice run of tomorrow's nuptials.

"Oh, come on now, Leah. Don't you see yourself settling down one day? Finding that special someone who will make you go all mushy inside?" I grinned.

"Yep, just officially barfed a little in my mouth. And no, I will never settle down. There isn't a man in the world who could handle all this," she said, waving her hands up and down her body.

"You don't think my buddy Declan could handle all...that?" I waved my finger up and down, mimicking her motions.

"Shhh!! We do not speak his name!" she said.

"Is he like Voldemort?"

"No, Dr. Dork. But I would just prefer to not talk about that specific member of the male species. Ever."

I gave her a hard look, as she wrapped her hands across her chest.

"He didn't hurt you, did he?" Leah and I weren't as close as Clare and Leah were, but I'd come to be very fond of the crazy blonde walking next to me. Declan was a good friend of mine, we'd grown up together, but if he'd hurt her, I'd call him on it. I'd add a few other things to the list as well, like asking where the fuck was he? It was a day before my wedding day and he was nowhere to be seen. My best friend Colin, his wife and newborn son had all flew in today to be here. My mom, who until recently was estranged, was here. Everyone who mattered to me was here. Except Declan. He hadn't spoken to me since the day I told him I had cancer. It's not like I was going to give it to him…He knew that right?

Jackass.

"No, he didn't hurt me. We had a good time. A very, very…very good time."

"Seriously, don't need details," I said, raising my hands up in defense.

"But that's all it was. I would prefer to go on with my life not ever talking about Declan James again. It was one night, and that's it. No use talking about it anymore."

Her lips were saying one thing, but her body language was saying something entirely different.

She looked edgy and pissed. Her arms wrapped around her chest, and her eyes narrowed in front of her like she was ready to shoot laser beams out of them at a moment's notice.

"Okaaay."

Women were weird. Like batshit crazy weird. And I was living with two of them now. My only prayer… and I didn't pray often…was that if Clare and I were blessed enough to have more children— for my sanity, please make it a boy.

CLARE

"Grandma Cece!" Maddie exclaimed, giggling and running over to meet Logan's mother, who gladly caught my daughter in her arms, burying her head in her hair like she'd been counting down the minutes until their reunion.

"I missed you, Sweetheart!" Cece said. "Did you get bigger? You did, didn't you?"

Maddie laughed, and squirmed when Cece's fingers started tickling all the right spots, although, to be fair, there really wasn't a bad spot. Every-where on Maddie was fair game when it came to tickling.

"She's eating like a horse, so it wouldn't surprise me if she's shot up about five feet since we were in New York," Logan said, coming up behind me. He wrapped his arms around my waist and placed a soft kiss on my bare shoulder.

His mother caught his sweet gesture and I saw the smile in her eyes.

"The other day, I ate all of my chicken nuggets, and I was still hungry. So, Logan gave me all of his and even his mashed potatoes. I love mashed potatoes. He even let me make a mashed potato snow man before I ate them."

Hearing my fiancé wasn't eating tugged at my nerves, but I promised I wouldn't nag him. He'd sworn he was fine, and things were okay. He'd said he was just getting used to the medicine and it would take time, but the part of me that had lost someone wanted to put him in a plastic bubble and force feed him just to make sure he was strong enough to take on anything.

I was marrying a doctor.

I had to keep reminding myself of that fact.

He wouldn't purposely hurt himself. Seeing the way he looked at Maddie and me, I knew he wouldn't risk his health. Not now. Not when he had so much to lose.

So I needed to do the impossible. I needed to trust fate, that cruel, twisted bitch who'd already taken so much from me. I needed to trust that he would fight this and would be here with me at the end, holding my hand, kissing my shoulder, just like he was today.

Because the alternative was just too hard to imagine.

After receiving a proper welcome from Maddie, Cece, or Cecelia as she was properly known, made her way around the room greeting everyone. She finally made her way back to us, and gave us both long, lingering hugs.

"I love you, Logan," she whispered as she held on to her son. So many years had been lost between them and I knew she was trying to make up for the time lost. For the time she'd wasted.

"I love you too, Mom."

Tears glistened in her eyes, and she nodded, giving me a small smile. She cupped my chin briefly before being dragged off by Maddie once again. We said our hellos to her new husband, Richard, and made our way around the room, greeting our other guests that had made it in that day.

"Dude, vasectomy. I'm telling you. Get one. Now," I heard Logan's best friend Colin say.

"It can't possibly be that bad, Colin. Millions of people have babies every day."

"I haven't slept in fucking days, Logan. Days. I swear that little monster is trying to make me slowly go insane. He's smart. Like freaky smart. I think he somehow knows when I'm about to fall asleep, because he'll pick that exact moment to scream bloody murder. My nerves are shot man."

I tried not to laugh. I really did.

"It will get easier, Colin. I promise," I said.

"I don't know, Clare. I think this is my punishment. I think this is what I get for trying to clone pure awesomeness—a baby demon."

Logan and I just stared blankly at him, completely unable to form words.

"What?" he said.

"I'm so telling your wife you just called your son a baby demon," Logan said.

"You wouldn't."

"Oh, I would. And you wouldn't be able to do a damn thing about it, because tomorrow's my wedding. That makes it like an unofficial holiday, so I guess I'm the unofficial king."

"What do you want?"

Colin must be really afraid of his wife if he was willing to strike up a bargain with Logan just to avoid the backlash. Of course, I'd seen Colin and Ella in action and part of me understood. They worked well together, but they were both very passionate. Colin was arrogant and full of himself and Ella was self-assured and independent. They both pretended not to need the other but they did. Badly.

"I want you to be the best damn best man in the history of best men. If there was an award for it, I'd want to see your face plastered on the top of a trophy. Got it?"

"Got it. Be awesome. I can do that."

"I have specifics."

"Of course you do," Colin sighed.

"When I need something, you're there. If Clare and I need to duck out for a few minutes….half an hour, you make excuses. If I need a good hiding spot, you find me one."

My eyebrows rose at this odd request. I gave him a look, and he grinned.

He leaned in, close to my ear and whispered, "Did you think I'd be able to wait all night to take my wife?"

Instant red flushed my face, and I turned away, trying to hide my obvious embarrassment. Colin was now grinning as well, and I pretty much wanted to die right then and there.

"Anything you want man, I'm there."

I was getting married tomorrow, and it was shaping up to be a very interesting day.

LOGAN

I had no idea she was going to speak, until she was tapping her fork against her wine glass to gather everyone's attention. We had decided not to give speeches. Too many emotions, and neither one of us wanted to break down in the middle of our rehearsal or reception. So, we were going to leave the speech making to everyone else, if they wanted. We still weren't sure we'd survive that so we weren't holding anyone to it. With lives like ours, celebrations went beyond champagne and fancy food. It was the ability to celebrate that was worth the celebration, and no one knew this better than the woman standing before me.

"Thank you all for coming. I know a lot of people say that at things like this, but I truly mean it. I know it was last minute and far away, but not a single one of you ever complained. Each one of you, the people who mean the most to us, happily took vacation days, did some last minute packing and hopped on planes to celebrate this special occasion, and it wouldn't be the same without you."

Clare briefly glanced down at me, giving me a faint smile. I took her delicate hand in mine, weaving our fingers together like I always did and smiled back.

"Life is full of unexpected surprises. Some good like the blessing of a child, and some not so good… like losing a loved one way too early."

She paused for a moment, gathering her thoughts and calming her emotions. I held on to her hand still, caressing her soft skin with the pad of my thumb.

"Logan is one of those surprises in life that takes

your breath away, leaving you completely awestruck by the enormity of the gift. But sometimes, wonderful, sweet and even incredibly sexy gifts are hard to accept."

Our small group chuckled, and I looked up to give her a quick grin.

"How do you comprehend such an amazing blessing, when your life has already been filled with them? This was the question I struggled with. When you've already been given so much, can you really take more? Many of you don't know this, but before Ethan died, he wrote me a letter. I was supposed to open it when I was ready, but until recently I didn't know what I was supposed to be ready for. In that letter, Ethan gave me my answer. Life is too short to worry about the why, or the how or the what-ifs. Love is a risk, there are no guarantees. But in the end, it is always, always worth it."

Through my very unmanly blurry eyes, I looked around to find an entire room of matching tear stained faces staring back at us.

"I'm sorry to make all of you cry, but before all the craziness of tomorrow, I wanted you all to know how much of a gift Logan is to my life. He has taught me how to remember without being sad, how to live again, and most importantly, how to love again. I couldn't have picked a better man to love my daughter and complete our family."

Clare then quietly sat in her seat, and our eyes met. Everyone else in the room disappeared.

"Thank you for walking into that exam room, and for being brave enough to take on two redheads for a lifetime. I love you."

The small amount of space that separated us was suddenly too much. I reached out, wrapping my hand around the back of her head and pulled gently until our foreheads touched. Her brilliant green eyed gaze bore into me, seeing the deepest parts of my soul.

"I love you, Clare."

I closed the gap, kissing the lips of the angel who would soon become mine in every way.

Chapter Eight

"*I* look like a peacock," I said, staring at the scary reflection of myself in the hotel salon.

"A very cute peacock," Leah amended, before asking, "What exactly did you tell the woman to do?"

"I told her I wanted an updo. Something classy."

"Well…I'm not sure I'd say it's classy, but it's sure something." I could see her trying to hold back a laugh.

Just about the time I was about to disown her as my best friend and maid of honor for laughing at me in my hour of need, Maddie came bouncing over. She'd just had her hair done, and of course, her hair was gorgeous. A pile of perfectly curled red ringlets flowed down her back. It was pinned at the sides with tiny sparkly pins that matched her coral colored dress.

"Mommy! Look how pretty I am!" she exclaimed.

"Oh baby! You look beautiful!" She twirled around and both Leah and I clapped and "oohed" and "ahhed" at the right times. She loved every minute of it.

After a few minutes of undivided attention, where she showed us her perfect hair, sparkly pins and every single detail of her dress and matching shoes, she looked up and paused.

"Mommy! Your hair! You look just like that lady on TV!"

Confused, I asked, "What lady?"

"The one who sings those songs that Aunt Leah loves that you won't let me sing?"

Trying to think back and remember the many inappropriate songs Leah listened to, I remembered a conversation I'd had with her a few weeks ago, when Leah and I were watching the MTV Music Video awards.

"Lady Gaga?" I asked.

"Yep! That lady has hair just like you!"

I gave Leah a panicked look and the laugh that she'd been previously holding back suddenly burst out of her like a volcano and she doubled over.

"Hey baby, why don't you go find Grammy and

see what her hair looks like?" I suggested, giving Leah a sideways evil glare.

"Okay, Mommy!" she said, skipping off in search of my mom.

"Oh my God. First, I'm going to kill you, and then I'm going to find someone to fix this bird's nest on top of my hair. No…scratch that. First, *you're* going to find someone to fix this…and *then* I'm going to kill you."

"Calm down, Clare-bear. It's going to be okay. I'm going to go find the manager, and we'll get this crazy disco stick disaster fixed and you'll be back to looking like you."

One hour, two hair stylists and several mimosas later…I had a brand new do. It was stunning. Leah had talked me out of an updo and we instead went with something more natural. Loose curls cascaded down my back and were pinned with small antique pearl clips that framed my face perfectly.

"You are a miracle worker, Leah." I said, staring at my own shocked expression in the mirror.

"Does this mean I've been forgiven?" she asked.

"What? Oh, yes. Definitely. You are redeemed. For another day."

"Well, good. Now, let's get you back to the bridal suite. We have a wedding dress to put on!" she practically squealed.

We all made our way back up to the suite, and it

was my turn to laugh when Leah, having had one too many mimosas, pretended to be my own wacky version of secret service, jumping ahead to check around corners, and clear hallways to protect her "asset" from the men. She was taking her maid of honor role very seriously and we managed to arrive upstairs without being seen by anyone.

As we entered the suite, we were greeted by my mother and Cece, who had an exuberant Maddie in her arms. She was telling her soon-to-be grandmother all about her adventures in the salon, and Cece was hanging on every word like it was the most important conversation in the world. Ella was in the corner rocking her little one, humming a soft lullaby. Her hair was curled and pinned to the side, just below her ear.

"Oh my, Sweetheart! You are a vision," my mother said.

"Mommy! What happened to your other hair?" Maddie asked, which caused us all to laugh.

"Well," I started, leaning down in front of her, "I decided I wasn't cool enough to have that hairdo, so we thought this might be more my style."

She gave me an appraising look, her eyes wandering up and down my long red locks, before she said, "You're right. It's much better."

I don't know if I was more relieved that she liked it or a little hurt that she agreed I wasn't cool enough. But either way, we were ready to move onto makeup, and that is where Leah came in. She was a wizard of all things cosmetic. She'd been doing my makeup for special events ever since we were old enough to have special events.

"Plant it right here," she said, pointing to an empty chair at the desk. It was a perfect spot, situated in front of a large mirror so I could watch as she did her work.

Half an hour later and with a little help from Ella, she was done. She'd done a beautiful job of making me look classy and sexy but not over the top. Just enough, with shimmery natural shadows and peach blush and gloss, and I looked radiant.

With Leah standing over my shoulder, our eyes locked and held in the mirror. I knew she was thinking about the last time she did my makeup for a major event—the day I married Ethan. Her lip quivered and my hand went up to my shoulder to grasp hers.

"I know," I said. It was all I had to say. I knew, like her, that we were all still grieving and always would be. I knew that this day was hard, even though there was so much joy. I knew this all because sometimes when a friendship goes beyond normal borders and you find a sister, rather than an ordinary friend, conversations aren't necessary.

"Well, let's get you married," Leah said, trying to steady her now shaky voice.

"Yes, let's do that," I agreed.

Both mothers gushed over my makeup, and complimented Leah on her fine job. She politely thanked them and we all made our way to my gown, which was still hanging in its bag by the closet.

"So Laura was telling me that your original dress was ruined?" Cece asked. She had obviously been caught up on the dress drama by my mom when they shared their hair appointments that morning. Both were sporting sophisticated updos that made them look regal and lovely. Their updos didn't resemble Lady Gaga at all.

"Yes, the airline ate it. But, it worked out well," I said, as I slid down the zipper and pulled the dress from its bag to a collective gasp.

"This one is much better."

"Oh my goodness, Clare," Cece said, at the same time my mother said, "Oh, sweetheart, you're going to be stunning!"

"Well, let's get it on me!" I exclaimed. The gown I'd chosen wasn't overly complicated which fit our outdoor wedding perfectly. It was vintage in style, with champagne satin underneath a beautiful lace overlay that flowed slightly behind me in an elegant train. A matching champagne colored satin bow completed the look and wrapped around my waist.

With everyone's help, minus Maddie who was jumping up and down shouting her Mommy was *the prettiest Mommy ever,* I was soon standing in front of the floor-length mirror in my gown.

"It's just…" Leah started.

"Perfect," I finished.

With teary eyes, Cece asked, "Do you have your something blue?"

Panic. Pure panic took over and I looked at everyone standing behind me with wide eyes.

"Oh my God. I completely forgot. Everything. The something old, the something new…I don't even have something blue! Is my marriage doomed?"

Leah's face curved into a smile and I seriously wanted to turn around and smack her for smiling in my time of need.

"Why are you smiling?" I nearly shouted.

"Logan knew you'd forget."

"What?"

"He knew you'd forget, with everything being so last minute and rushed. He knew this, so he took care of everything and asked me to deliver the goods to you."

"And you're just deciding to tell me now?" I asked.

"It was worth that face, that's for sure."

As I was silently chanting *I love my best friend, I love my best friend* in my head, Leah ushered me over to a plush chair where I sat down while she gathered whatever it was that Logan had planned.

She took a seat on the sofa adjacent to me and began.

"He wrote a letter. Do you want to read it, or shall I?"

Fearing I wouldn't make it through reading the letter myself, I gave her the go ahead, and she began.

> "Clare,
>
> Today you will become my wife, and I will give my sacred vow to always take care of you and Maddie. It is my honor and I will spend every day of my life trying to prove I'm worthy of the task. Ever since the day I met you, I've wanted to protect you from everything that may harm you, or cause you pain or stress. I know this impromptu wedding has been less than ideal, and if the circumstances were different, we would have had time to plan something different.
>
> In all the craziness, I knew you would forget the small things. It is your nature to focus on everyone else's needs—Maddie's and mine....the guests. I knew you'd eventually realize the small traditional elements of the wedding you'd overlooked and by then it would

Leah handed me the lace handkerchief I'd always seen laying in my mother's cedar chest when I was growing up. I'd never been allowed to touch it, knowing it was delicate and old. I tried to hold back the tears as I felt it in my grasp for the first time. I glanced up and found my mom. She had the same teary eyed expression on her face, and I met her halfway, jumping from the chair to fall into her arms.

"I love you, sweetheart."

"I love you, too, Mama."

"Love that man with everything you have, for as long as you have, baby girl."

"I will, Mama."

With my handkerchief clutched between my fingers, I settled back into my chair and braced for whatever else Logan had in store for me.

"Are you ready?" Leah asked, and I just nodded.

"For your something new, I didn't need any assistance at all. I had everything I needed, because your something new is me! So, you'll have to wait until later to put me on. Our love is still young and new, and I will spend every day of my life making sure the love we feel for each other when we take our vows not only is the same but only grows stronger and deeper."

I laughed, and shook my head.
"Goofball," Leah said as we all laughed.
"Sweet goofball."

"For your something borrowed, I asked my mother to help out. As you know, my mother used to be quite the hoarder of labels and anything designer. But, when she met Richard, she gave it all up, keeping only a few things that had sentimental value to her. The pearl earrings she is lending you today is one of those pieces."

Cece came forward then and handed me a box.

"These were handed down to me by my mother, and were always very special to me. It would be an honor if you wore them on the day you married my son."

I simply nodded, the lump in my throat now reaching epic proportions. I wasn't going to survive the day. I really hoped whatever makeup Leah put on me was hurricane proof because I saw a lot of tears in my future.

She opened the box and enclosed where a beautiful set of pearl earring that matched my gown beautifully.

"Thank you, Cece," I said.

"From today on, you call me Mom."

We came together in a hug and silently thanked the man who had tamed the untamable woman and given Logan his mother back.

"Okay, Leah…how much more? I don't know if my makeup can handle more."

"Your makeup is just fine, and I will be there to touch it up if needed, so calm down. There's just one more thing and I think you're going to like it," she said with a wicked grin.

"For your something blue, I considered doing the blue garter thing, which is both traditional and sexy, but then I decided to take it one step further. So, I went shopping,

and forgive me....my one step further went a little crazy. But picturing you in blue on our wedding night kind of drove me insane. Enjoy, and I'll see you soon. I love you—Logan."

I gave Leah a look, and asked, "Do I need to send my mother out of the room?"

"Oh please, Sweetheart. Like I didn't know why you two were late last night," my mother said with a flick of the wrist.

"Oh my God, I'm going to go in the corner and die now," I said, as Leah muffled a laugh.

"Oh, come on. It's only lingerie. It's not like your mom hasn't owned a thong or two," Leah said.

I gave her a hard look and motioned over to Maddie who was busy reading a book on the floor, completely oblivious to our conversation. Thank God.

"First of all—Maddie is right there. Second of all —gross."

"You know, you always use Maddie as an excuse, but ninety percent of the time, she's never paying attention when I'm talking, so it's a really lame excuse."

I opened my mouth to offer a rebuttal, but she was actually right. How did that happen? I wonder if Leah was more observant than I thought. *Nah.*

"So, let's see this lingerie!" Cece exclaimed and I

tried not to think about the fact my mother and soon-to-be mother in law were getting excited over my wedding night lingerie.

Leah pulled out an elegantly wrapped package and waited and watched as I unwrapped it.

"Oh, hurry the hell up, Clare!" she huffed as I carefully opened the gift.

"The wrapping paper is pretty!"

"And you're going to take it home with you?" she asked.

"Well, no…"

"So, then…hurry! Otherwise, you're going to be late for your own wedding!"

"Okay, okay!"

I hurried up and had the box opened and was face to face with the most gorgeous undergarments I'd ever seen.

"These did not come from Victoria's Secret," I said.

"No. No, they did not," was all Leah could manage. I think I heard Ella say *holy shit* under her breath at the same time.

There must have been thousands of dollars of lingerie in there. A beautiful dark blue satin and lace corset with a matching blue thong lay amongst layers of tissue paper. White stockings with little blue bows and, of course, a blue garter was also in there.

"You know what this means?" Leah said.

"My fiancé has a shopping problem?"

"Nope, we've got to strip you down again and get you all sexified."

Awesome...putting on the lingerie I will wear on my wedding night...with my mom and new mother-in-law.

Great way to bond.

LOGAN

I was quickly discovering that being the groom on the day of a wedding was vastly different than being the bride. As Clare was being primped and pampered, going from appointment to appointment doing whatever it was that women did for these types of things, I was sitting in the bar with the guys.

"We really should have planned this day out a bit better," Colin said, taking a swig from his half empty beer.

"When I woke up this morning and realized I had an entire day with nothing to do, I thought we had it made. But dude, this is fucking boring. I'd rather be golfing."

I hated golfing. It was what rich people did to

appear outdoorsy, and I'd been around it my entire life. My father was a huge golfer, and I had spent many summers caged up in a golf cart following him around while he tried to explain the virtues of the game.

"Golf is important Logan. I've made many important business deals over a good game of golf," he'd said. *Yeah, whatever.*

The fact that I'd rather be out hitting golf balls spoke volumes of the depth of my boredom.

"How long does it take to get ready for a wedding?" I asked.

"Really fucking long," Colin answered, "Don't you remember doing this same damn thing at my wedding? Those girls were gone for years getting ready. Damn if I couldn't tell the difference when she walked down the aisle either."

I gave him a look, the look I'd been giving him for years that told him he was crossing the line into his douchebag alter-ego. Colin and I had been best friends since college and I'd quickly learned he was cocky, self-assured and outspoken. Sometimes the combination of those got out of hand, and he went from being what women would classify as cute and cocky to instant jackass.

"No, man…I don't mean it like that. I just meant that she was already gorgeous. She could have spent an entire week getting herself pampered and ready to walk down that aisle, or she could have showed up in a paper sack, and I still would have thought she was the most beautiful woman in the world."

"Damn, Colin. I don't think I've ever heard you say something so poetic before in my entire life. Garrett—write this down," I said, motioning to my soon-to-be brother in law who was also nursing a beer next to us. "Colin just said something heartfelt and touchy-feely. I want evidence."

Garrett just shook his head and grinned.

"So, 'Colin the Wise', what last words of wisdom do you have for me before I take my vows?"

He gave me a doubtful look, "You seriously want me to give you advice…about marriage?"

"Well, it's not like we have anything else to do," I said, motioning to the rest of the bar which was completely empty except for the three of us. Make that four. I greeted my future father in law as he strolled in, taking a seat next to his son. He ordered a beer and then turned to our small group.

"Afternoon, gentlemen. What did I miss?" he asked.

"Colin was about to give me marriage advice," I answered, pointing to Colin who grinned like an asshole.

"This should be good," Mr. Finnegan, or Tom as he liked to be called, said. We all chuckled and agreed.

"Hey! For your information, I am a damn good husband. It's not easy, and it's not always hearts and flowers, but if you find the right woman, like Ella….it's worth it. Every damn minute. And if you're really lucky, she'll give you the greatest gift imaginable….a mini version of the two of you all mushed together. It's incredible."

"You had me," I said, clutching my chest, "right here….until you starting talking about mush, and then I got lost."

"Shut up Logan! You asked for wisdom and there it is. Work at it, every day. They may drive you crazy, run you ragged and send your mind spinning, but one look from Ella and I'm a goner. Still. She's it for me, and I will spend every day of my life reminding her that I'm the same for her."

"That was actually pretty good Colin. I'm mighty impressed," Tom said.

"Me, too. Who knew you were such a softy under all that crap," I joked. I knew he loved his wife. He'd loved her since the moment he saw her enter the crowded bar we'd be hanging out at all those years ago. He'd told me that night she was his future wife. I thought he was just drunk, but damned if he didn't do it.

"Well, I have a reputation to uphold. Can't let everyone know what lies beneath all this," he said, making a grand sweeping gesture over his physique. We all groaned, and I asked if he was finished.

"One more thing. Don't leave the toilet seat up. They hate that."

I shook my head and laughed and we all clanked our glasses together in a half-assed toast. I checked my watch and swore time had frozen. Not even an hour had passed.

Longest. Day. Ever.

"How about you, Mr. Finnegan," Colin said, "Got any advice for my boy Logan?"

He was silent for a moment, staring into the empty beer glass in front of him.

"Never go to bed angry and don't sweat the small stuff. You never know what tomorrow will bring, and life is too short to worry about things that don't matter. When I had my stroke, do you think I sat in that hospital bed worrying about whether the house chores would be done or the trash would be taken out? No, I thought about my wife and children and how much I wanted to fight so I could spend another day with them by side. You have a fight ahead of you Logan, don't waste breath on things that aren't worthy of it."

"Thank you," was all I could manage. I stuck out my hand for a handshake but he instead pulled me into a bear hug. I'd never had a loving father. I didn't know how to interact with one. Tom, along with

Clare and the rest of her family, were showing me what it was like to have a family and a place to call home.

My future was bright and full of infinite possibilities because of her, and if the clock ever decided to move again, she would be my wife in just a few short hours. Nothing could keep me down. Not even cancer.

Chapter Ten

"Breathe, just breathe," I chanted. My heart was running a marathon in my chest and I was convinced it would soon explode from my ribs roadrunner style, headed straight for the altar to get to Logan first.

Now that I had that picture in my head, it was nearly as romantic as I had originally thought.

"Are you nervous?" Leah asked, standing beside me in her knee-length coral dress that accented her bronze skin and honey blonde hair perfectly.

"No, I'm ready. Like really ready. Why are we still back here?"

She snorted before answering. "Because you still have fifteen minutes before the ceremony is supposed to start. You have to allow the rest of the guests to be seated."

"What guests?" I asked impatiently. "The only guests that are here are family, and the wedding party. How can they not all be seated by now?" I huffed.

"Alright, Clare-bear, let's re-do your makeup and primp a little. We need to get your mind off the clock, otherwise you're going to explode."

I nodded in agreement. I really was going to explode. Logan was out there in his tan suit, probably standing at the altar with the deep blue ocean serving as a backdrop behind him. He was waiting for me, and I didn't want to make him wait anymore. I wanted to barrel down that aisle and hear the minister say *husband and wife* so I could scream to the world that he was all mine.

Leah dabbed, blotted and glossed my lips until she was satisfied, and then put all of her tools away in her little clutch bag that she'd stowed just inside the door we were about to walk out of. The wedding was not on the beach, but it was as close as we could get without having to make all our guests sink in the sand with their nice shoes on. The hotel had a beautiful garden patio with an almost surround view of the ocean. At the very edge was a grassy area where we'd set up chairs and a gorgeous flower covered altar. Nothing else was needed. The view took care of the rest.

Everyone else was either seated or being seated. It was just Leah, Ella, Maddie and me. We all grasped hands and tried not to cry.

"I love you guys," I said.

"We love you, too, babe," Ella said. "Thank you for loving Logan, and for bringing him back to us. You've completed him, and I've never seen him so full of life."

I pulled her into my arms and we hugged. I was so grateful Logan had friends that had cared for him through everything. Even in his darkest points when he pushed everyone away, Colin and Ella had stayed.

I kneeled down to my beautiful daughter who was just as excited as me, but when she jumped up and down, it was cute. Kids got off so easy.

"Are you excited baby?" I asked, and she gave me a huge nod, over exaggerating every movement.

"After you're married, can I call Logan my Daddy? Do you think Daddy would be mad?"

The tears I'd been trying to hold back let loose down my cheek and I pulled her into my arms.

"No, baby. I think Daddy would love that. Logan too. No one said you couldn't have two daddies, right?"

She pulled back and nodded, "Right. I can't wait to tell him!"

I turned to Leah who was holding back tears. She was my rock. She'd been with my almost every day of my life, for as long as I could remember. She'd been my protector, the sister I never had, and the shoulder I needed when everything fell apart.

"I wouldn't be here without you. You know that, right?" I said.

"You would have found your way eventually. I just gave you the push you needed to get you here quicker. The love you and Logan share isn't a coincidence. I'm convinced you would have found each other over and over until you realized you were destined for each other."

Squeezing her hand, I asked, "And what about you? You don't need to put your life on hold for me anymore. Start living again, Leah."

She gave a faint smile that didn't quite reach her eyes, "I will, Clare-bear. I am. Don't worry about me today."

After one last hug, the coordinator the hotel provided came by and gave us the go-ahead.

It was time.

Maddie went first, holding her little basket of flowers. She was very serious about her flower girl duties and held off on dropping any petals until the right time.

Ella went next, clutching her small bouquet of island flowers in her hand.

Before Leah was given her go-ahead, she turned around, gave me a quick wink and a kiss on the cheek, and she was gone.

"Didn't think you were going to walk down that aisle without your old man, did you?" my father said, coming to stand beside me at just the right time.

"I knew you'd make it," I said, giving him a sideways grin.

"I knew you three needed some girly time, so I hung back in the hallway. But now you're all mine. I love you, baby girl."

My lip quivered and every minute spent with my father in my childhood came roaring back. The skinned knees when he was teaching me to ride my bike, the yelling matches and frustration when I got behind the wheel for the first time, and that moment when he caught Ethan and I in the kitchen and realized I wasn't his little girl anymore.

"I love you too, Daddy."

He held out his arm and I took it and we were on our way, down the path toward Logan and my future.

LOGAN

"Breathe, just breathe," I silently chanted, as I caught my first glimpse of Clare walking down the path with her father.

She was a vision. Covered in lace that fit her like a glove, her dress blended old with new seamlessly. She had left her hair down and under the sun, it shimmered with the fiery red glow I loved. There was too much of her to take in at once, and my eyes were everywhere, trying to drink in every detail. I wanted to remember everything, sear it into my memory so I'd never forget the emotions that were welling up inside me.

"Marry Me" by Train was being strummed softly by a lone guitarist as she came towards me. Our eyes locked and everyone disappeared. I barely noticed when her father placed her hand in mine, still unable to believe this was my life. This woman was here. To marry me.

I heard a soft chuckle and I looked up briefly to see Tom shaking his head and taking his seat beside his wife.

The minister cleared his throat and Clare and I finally tore our eyes apart and turned our attention to him.

"I think we should begin, don't you?" he asked, and Clare and I both looked at each other and nodded. Apparently the world disappearing around us hadn't gone unnoticed.

"I do. I absolutely do," I said.

"I haven't gotten to that part yet," he laughed.

"Well, then hurry up," I joked, which earned a few laughs from the guests.

The minister welcomed everyone and began with a reading. It was a quote or a passage about love. I honestly didn't listen. It was something Clare and I had picked out and I remember it being beautiful. But seriously, how could I focus on anything when Clare was standing in front of me?

I did hear him say *vows*, and that's when I started to pay attention.

"Clare and Logan have chosen to recite their own vows, and will do so now." He turned to Clare and gave her the go ahead. She nodded, turned back to me and gave me that shy smile I'd fallen in love with.

"You once said you didn't think you were capable of love—that somehow that ability was lost on you. You were so afraid to let us in, scared that you wouldn't be able to give back what we could so freely offer. But I've never known anyone more capable of love than you Logan. It shines through in everything you do, and there is no one on this earth I would rather be binding myself to than you."

I didn't deserve her. Standing there, hearing her speak, I knew she was so much more than I deserved and exactly what I needed. She completed me in every way.

She took a deep breath and continued, "I promise to love you a little bit more each and every day. I promise to hold your hand, even when we're old and frail. I vow that no matter what life hands us, I will stand by your side, ready and willing to face the challenges that lie ahead. I will always try to make you laugh and promise to share my dessert with you —maybe." Her lip curved into a small smile, and she laughed which only made her more beautiful.

"But more than anything, Logan, I promise you will always have me. All of me. Everything I have is yours. You are my family, my future and my forever."

I wanted to kiss her. I'd never wanted to kiss her more, but before I had the chance, a throat was clearing again and it was my turn. My turn to pledge myself to this woman. For eternity, and I couldn't wait.

"I should have gone first. I should have gone first because I can barely speak after that. I've forgotten everything I was going to say. You rendered me speechless and I have been in a constant state of awe since the moment I looked into these mystically green eyes. You bewitch me, captivate me, and propel me to be a better person. I was an empty shell until you showed me what love was."

I had written vows, and memorized them. It had taken me days, and I done nothing this morning but pace my hotel room reciting them. And now, nothing. I was just a rambling, gushing mess of words. But, it wasn't pretty speeches and memorization that made a vow. It was what came from the heart, and suddenly forgetting my page-long vows didn't seem so bad.

"I promise to always make you pizza whenever you want. I will never leave the house without first kissing you goodbye and promising chocolate on my return. I will always put you and Maddie first in my life—you two are my life. I vow to spend every day of my life proving to you that the promises you just made to me were worth it—that we're worth it. I promise to always play the guitar for you when you have trouble falling asleep. I will never sweat the small stuff or allow the sun to set with anger in our bed." I gave Tom a meaningful look and he nodded. Repeating the words she said to me, I said, "You are my family, my future and my forever….and I will walk with you wherever this crazy road called life may take us."

Her hands tightened around mine and tiny tears trickled down her cheek. I reached up and gently wiped them away.

"Now that Clare and Logan have said their vows, they will now exchange rings. Rings are a symbolic representation of the love between a husband and wife. As a ring has no beginning or end, your lives are now joined in one unbroken circle, for love that is given comes back around again. May these rings you exchange today always remind you of the vows you have taken today and of the promises that have been made."

We had no ring bearer, so Colin and Leah served as our official keeper of the rings. Leah stepped forward and handed Clare my ring, and gave us a teary eyed wink.

Clare took the ring in her right hand and positioned it over my ring finger before saying, "With this ring, I give you my heart, soul and unending love. With this ring, I marry you."

She slipped the cool platinum band down my ring finger, and our eyes locked. It slid into place and I felt like a missing piece of my soul had just returned.

Colin tapped my shoulder and handed me the ring that I would place on Clare's finger. It was simple and handmade to match her antique wedding engagement ring. Repeating the same process, I took her left hand and positioned the ring and said, " With this ring, I give you my heart, soul and unending love. With this ring, I marry you."

Her eyes followed my movements as I slid her wedding ring down her slim finger.

"Now that they have recited vows and exchanged rings, I only have one thing left to do," the minister said and I grinned.

"You have made lifelong promises of love and faithfulness today, sealing yourselves to each other for all the days of your life. By the power vested in me, I now pronounce you husband and wife."

Turning to me, who was no doubt grinning like a fool, he said, "You may now kiss your bride."

He didn't have to tell me twice. I closed the small gap that separated us and kissed my wife. Our lips met and, like every time I kissed Clare, it felt like the first time. I wove my fingers into her hair and deepened our kiss, forgetting that there were about fifteen people around us, including my brand new mother- and father-in-law.

Better save some of that for later.

I reluctantly pulled away, just enough that our foreheads still touched, and I could feel her damp cheeks against mine.

Laughing slightly, our minister said, "May I introduce, for the first time, Mr. And Mrs. Logan Matthews!"

I liked the sound of that.

Chapter Eleven

I was really starting to regret the idea of a reception.

I loved my family and friends, but honestly…I wanted them all gone. Now.

Logan and I were married. *Finally.*

I wanted nothing more than just him and me and an endless amount of time to spend naked in a bed.

But I was the one who wanted a reception. Logan had said he didn't want anything after we said I do except me. Naked. I'd told him we needed to respect our family who'd flown out for the event, so he grumbled and agreed. We'd planned a small reception, opting out of many of the traditional things done at a larger wedding. Just a meal and cake was on the schedule for tonight, but I knew it would still be forever before we got out of here.

I hated that he was right all the time.

I didn't have a watch, but I was assuming it would be at least three hours before we could get out of here. After that, we had an entire week of vacation. We weren't calling it a honeymoon, because we had decided to include Maddie. The grandparents had all offered to take her for a week, but this had originally been our vacation, until we switched into our wedding celebration. We didn't want to kick her out of her own vacation. Plus, we were a new family and Logan was a new father. We not only needed time as a couple, but time as a family.

So, we were having a honeymoon, plus one. We could have a real honeymoon later. We still had our own bedroom and had activities planned for Maddie so we could have alone time when we needed it, but this felt right. We didn't know what our lives would be like in the next few months, and spending as much time together as possible sounded like the best option.

"I was right, wasn't I?" Logan whispered into my ear, returning with a glass of champagne from the bar.

"About what, dear husband?" I asked innocently.

"Mmm...say it again," he growled.

"Husband?"

"Yes." He wrapped his arms around my hips and pulled me forward. "I like that. *A lot.*"

"I can tell," I said, sliding my hand down his backside.

"Clare…," he warned.

"Yes, husband?"

"That's it. Meet me in the hallway, just over there," he said, pointing to my right, "In three minutes. Three minutes Clare."

I looked at him a bit amused. "Where are you going?"

"I'm going to cash in a favor."

Before I could ask him anymore, he was gone.

I didn't have a watch. How the hell was I supposed to tell when it'd been three minutes? I started counting in my head, *one-one-thousand, two-one-thousand….*and made my way around the small room, smiling and hugging as I continued to count in my head. I was just hoping no one asked me anything, otherwise I'd lose count. I was up to eight-nine.

"Honey, where did Logan run off to?" my mother asked, breaking my concentration.

Crap.

"Oh, um…I don't know. Probably to loosen up his tie, or check on the hotel room maybe?"

Had it been three minutes yet?

"Ah yes. We moved some of Maddie's things into

our suite for the night, so she's all set. Are you two staying in the honeymoon suite?"

"Yes. I told Logan it wasn't necessary. We already had a room...two actually. But he insisted, so I relented."

"Well I'm sure it will be perfect."

"Yes, it will be," I said, just as I saw Logan dart his head in and search the room. His gaze settled on me and I knew my three minutes were up.

"I'll be right back, Mom," I said, not bothering to hear what she said after that. The look Logan had just given me was scorching and I had to hold myself back from running out of the room.

Without causing too much of a scene, and being sure I said hello to everyone as I passed, I made my way toward the exit. Just as I was about to make my disappearing act, I ran head first into a brick wall.

I heard a chuckle. "Looks like you're ditching your own party, Big Sis," Garrett said.

I blushed and bit my lip, glancing around in hopes no one had noticed.

"I was just going to...." I stumbled on my words, trying to think up an excuse.

Garrett gave me a knowing grin, his green eyes glowing with mischief. A perfect match set to my own. It was something we'd both inherited from my mother.

"It's cool, Clare. I don't want to know," he said, shaking his head and holding up his hands in defeat.

"I'm happy for you, Sis. You deserve it."

"Thank you Garrett. That means a lot. Maybe we'll be doing the same thing at your wedding a few years from now? I promise I'll let you go quietly into the hallway, too," I joked.

His eyes went glassy and he turned away.

"Yeah, maybe."

He gave me another quick hug and told me to make my getaway while I still could. I ducked into the hallway and was immediately grabbed around the waist and pushed against the wall.

"It's been more than three minutes," Logan growled.

"I don't have a watch," I answered, holding up my wrist which only had a small strand of pearls circling it.

"Come on," he said, taking my hand in his and pulling me towards a closed door down the hall.

"Where are we going?"

We reached the door, and he quietly opened it and we ducked inside. It was the grand ballroom, dark and unused, since Logan had rented out the entire hotel.

"I can't wait another minute, Clare. I need to have my hands on you. Seeing you in that dress...

knowing that you're finally my wife. It's driving me insane."

He lifted me up and set me down on one of the round tables that were scattered around the room.

"What if someone comes in here?" I asked, biting my lip and totally loving the idea of doing something naughty.

"Believe me, no one's coming in here. Colin's making sure of that."

My eyes widened. "You don't mean he's out there," I said, pointing to the door, "standing watch?"

"What? No! Do you think I'd let that horn dog anywhere near here? He's paying off the staff."

"Oh," I said, smiling. "Well, how exactly are you going to get me out of this dress without me looking like a train wreck when we go back in?"

He flashed me a wolfish grin. "Who said I was going to take off the dress? I am definitely keeping the dress on. For now."

He stood between my legs and pulled me close, leaning down to kiss my lips. He was gentle at first, but became more urgent and heated. He fisted my hair and slanted my head so he could deepen the kiss. Moving down my neck, he kissed my collarbone and shoulder.

"Lie back," he commanded.

I did as I was told, and leaned back until my back hit the table top. His hands flitted down my curves, over my hips until he knelt and they found the hem of my dress. He lifted it and examined my champagne high heels.

"Nice." His eyes traveled to my legs. "Are these the stockings I bought for you?" he asked, his eyes quickly traveling up to meet mine in question.

"Yes," I answered.

He wrapped his fingers around my ankles and slowly started sliding his hands up until the found my hip and the lace top of the stockings where the blue garter was.

Logan stood, pushing my skirt up as he did.

"Christ. That's got to be the best money I've ever spent."

"And you haven't even seen all of it yet," I reminded him.

"Don't tempt me Clare. We need to keep you presentable for the family," he grinned.

Running his hands up my thighs, he paused. "I was just going to make you come because we don't have a lot of time. But seeing you like this, all spread out before me like a fucking platter? Now all I want to do is bury myself in you."

I pushed up to my elbows and gave him a challenging look.

"Then what's stopping you?"

He growled and suddenly I was in the air. My

legs wrapped around his waist seconds before he pushed us against the wall opposite of where we'd come in.

My skirt was gathered around my hips, and I heard the telltale sound of Logan's zipper and belt. All my insides went tight in anticipation as his hand slid up my thigh to push aside my lacy blue thong.

"We're going to consummate our marriage in an empty ballroom, standing against a wall, with our family down the hall. You okay with that?"

I could feel him hard and ready against me, waiting for my answer.

"Yes, Logan. God, yes," I managed to say as he plunged into my slick core.

I muffled my cries and moans against his shoulder as he pumped in and out, filling me completely with every stroke.

"I love you. So fucking much," he said roughly, slamming into my body harder. I could feel the orgasm building in my belly, swirly and twirling in my body like a tornado. His eyes focused on mine and he must have seen it in my eyes, because he took my mouth seconds before I cried out my orgasm, muting the sounds with our kiss.

One hand snaked around my body and found my bare ass. As he braced us against the wall with the other, he pulled me closer. His strokes were fast and uncontrolled, and within seconds his eyes glazed over and he gave a guttural moan as he came.

Still panting and in our post-coital haze, both of us jumped when there was a knock on the door.

"Logan!" Colin whispered.

"What the fuck do you want, man?" He suddenly looked down to make sure I was covered in case Colin was dumb enough to walk in. I really hoped he wasn't.

"They're starting to notice you guys are gone. Might want to hurry things along," he laughed.

"All right, thanks."

We turned to each other and couldn't help but laugh a little.

"Guess we better go before we get busted with our pants down!" Logan said.

We laughed and redressed each other, and headed back to our reception, hoping to hell that we didn't look like we'd just been shagging down the hall.

LOGAN

Dinner passed in a blur. I think we had chicken, or pork?

There were so many people talking to us, I honestly didn't have a chance to eat anyway, so it could have been lasagna for all I know.

All I could think about, in between answering questions about our "honeymoon" and our decision to sell Clare's house and move into mine, was the time we'd spent in that ballroom.

Visions of Clare lying on that table flashed before my eyes. Her hair fanned out in every direction like a whimsical goddess. The touch of her skin as I held her and slid inside her for the first time as husband and wife. The look in her eyes as she came.

Then it hit me. I'd taken my wife for the first time in a dark ballroom, fully clothed, backed up against a wall. I was an animal. I looked over in her direction and took her hand. She caught my eye and smiled, a faint blush spreading across her face.

I should have waited. Taken her slowly and lovingly. Stripped her down and spent hours kissing every inch of her skin. Instead, I'd taken her fast and hard, slamming her and that stunning wedding gown into a wall.

I suddenly had this overwhelming desire to show her exactly how much I treasured, loved and adored her. Maybe it was the whole cancer thing or just the high of getting married, but I decided to be spontaneous.

Rising from my seat, I gently kissed her temple. "I'm going to run up to the room and grab something. I'll be right back."

She gave me a confused look but just nodded and said okay.

Within fifteen minutes, I was walking back into the reception having completed my task.

Leah spotted me first, and her lips upturned into a smile.

"Hey, Superman, are you going to serenade me?"

Clare turned and saw my guitar slung over my shoulder and her eyes widened in surprise.

"No, I'm going to serenade my wife," I said with a grin.

The hotel staff was just about done setting up the impromptu stage, putting together a microphone and amp they had stored for larger weddings and business meetings.

All eyes were on me now as I set up, pulling my guitar out and taking a seat. I plugged everything in and then looked up to find Clare's green eyes staring back at me. I wasn't much of a performer. I played for myself, so I took a deep breath and tried to focus.

"I hadn't planned on entertaining everyone tonight, but one of Clare's favorite things lately has been listening to me play the guitar. So, today…on our wedding day, I wanted to sing her something special."

It had been a song I'd been working on for a while now. I'd heard it on her iPod a few weeks ago and I knew she loved the band, but probably didn't know I knew.

I started strumming the opening of "I'm Yours" by The Script and her eyes sparked in recognition.

Leaning into the microphone, I sang each word like they were written for her.

When I finished, there wasn't a dry eye in the house. Except for Maddie who came bounding up to me and jumped in my lap the moment I set the guitar down.

"I liked that song. It's pretty." she said.

"It is. A pretty song for your pretty mommy."

Clare came up to us, her eyes still wet from tears and she kneeled down in front of us, completing our new little family.

"You married my Mommy."

"Yes, I did," I answered, grinning at Clare.

"Mommy said that means I can call you Daddy."

Clare smiled and my full attention turned to Maddie who was looking at me with her big brown eyes. I couldn't put words together fast enough so I just nodded.

"So, can I call you Daddy now?"

Still nodding, I choked out a yes and pulled her to me. She'd been my daughter since the moment I committed myself to Clare, but this? This was more than I ever expected. I never wanted to replace the father she lost, but I also didn't want to go through life being known as *Logan, the stepfather.*

Tears I couldn't contain anymore broke free and I felt Clare lean in to join us. I pulled my two girls closer, and thanked every deity known to man for bringing them into my life.

Chapter Twelve

CLARE

After cake, which we very nicely fed to each other, and many well wishes later, we were set free. Maddie gave us hugs and said she was sorry she was leaving us to spend the night with Grandma and Grandpa. We laughed and told her it was okay and we'd survive one night without her.

As soon as we made our way up to the top floor and into our extravagant honeymoon suite, I gasped. He'd had the entire room covered in flickering candles and roses.

"You're crazy."

"Yes. Maybe a little," he said, "But only about you."

"This is over the top."

"I'm trying to make up for earlier."

"What do you mean?" I asked, confused.

He pulled me towards the bed, which was covered in red rose petals. There was a bucket of champagne chilling in the corner, and chocolate covered strawberries on the windowsill.

"I wanted every moment of today to be special for you. When we came together for the first time as husband and wife, I wanted you to know exactly how much I love you. I wanted to spend hours worshiping you and loving every part of you."

"So, you're worried that I'm going to look back and remember our first time as less than ideal?"

He cringed and nodded, "Yes, basically."

I pushed him down on the rose covered bed. He looked a bit startled but quickly grinned.

"The only thing that will make this night less than ideal is if you don't continue what you started in that ballroom and take me right now."

"Yes, Ma'am."

"Yes, what?" I asked, as he stood and slowly walked behind me.

"Yes, Mrs. Matthews," he whispered in my ear and began making quick work of the buttons and sash of my dress.

He rotated me around, brushing his hands around my waist as I turned until we were once again facing each other.

"You're so beautiful," he said. His fingers slipped

under the fabric of my dress at the nape of my neck and gently began pulling. When his eyes collided with the lacy top of my blue corset, he sucked in a breath and his hand dug into my hip.

It really was a beautiful work of art. Sapphire blue and ivory colored lace, with tiny pearls scattered everywhere. The fact that it made my breasts look like a million bucks didn't hurt either. Garter belts and matching stockings finished the look.

After Leah had helped me out of my wedding dress and into this, I'd stood in front of the floor length mirror in awe. I didn't even care that both my mother and Logan's mother were behind me. I was freaking hot.

And by the looks my husband was giving me, I'd say he agreed.

"Jesus," he breathed, as the last of my gown hit the floor, and he eyes went everywhere, roaming over every inch of my body.

"Turn around. Slowly," he ordered. His voice had dropped to that sexy tone I loved, and my stomach clenched in anticipation.

I made a slow circle, placing my hands on my hips and pivoting seductively so he could see all of me.

Before I'd even made it all the way back around, Logan was throwing off his suit jacket, tugging at his tie and tossing it to the ground. His eyes were wild by the time he looked up and zeroed in on me. It was hot.

He undid his cufflinks, followed by the buttons of his shirt, letting it hang freely to the sides which exposed his chest and perfect abs. He smirked, knowing I was loving what was in front of me, and continued his slow strip tease. His shirt hit the floor, and then in a rush, he made quick work of everything else, leaving only him standing in front of me.

My husband was so sexy.

Logan stalked towards me, backing us up until my thighs hit the bed. He gently wrapped his arms around my waist and lifted me, placing me under him on the bed.

"I knew the moment I walked into that exam room, my life had changed. You gave me a reason… two reasons to live," he said, brushing his hand down my thigh, as he kissed my neck.

He did this for what seemed like hours—running his hands up and down my body, kissing me everywhere as he whispered endearments and promises in my ear. By the time his fingertips reached the waistband of my thong, I was practically writhing in need.

"Logan…I need…," I started.

"I know," he said, as he slipped his finger inside me and flicked my clit. My hips shot forward and I let out a low moan.

"I think my wife likes that," he chuckled, "Let's see what else she likes."

My thong slid down my thighs and joined my gown on the floor.

"Mmm…this is a good look for you," he said as he pushed my legs forward and apart, exposing me completely. "Yes, a very good look."

He scooted down the bed until he was kneeling in front of it, and I nearly whimpered as I waited, knowing what would come next.

"Wrap those legs around my head Clare."

I did as I was instructed, watching as his hands moved up and down my thighs as I wrapped them around his head. His eyes were darker, like clouds right before a storm.

I criss-crossed my heels at the nape of his neck and he didn't waste any time, making me cry out as his mouth made its first contact with my core.

He licked and worshiped me with his mouth and within minutes, I was climaxing, pulling at his hair as I screamed his name. "Oh Logan, yes!"

He crawled up my body, and I reveled in the feel of his skin brushing against mine.

"I love seeing you in this, but I think it's time for it to go," he said seductively, reaching down to separate my garter belt from my stockings with an expert flick of his wrist. He repeated the process on the other side and then slowly slid the stockings down my legs, stopping only to remove my shoes.

He returned, hovering over me, as he removed my corset, taking time to undo every tiny fastening with care. Apparently he didn't want to ruin this piece of clothing. It didn't stop him from tossing it in the growing pile on the floor however.

"Finally, nothing but you," he said, before leaning down to brush his lips over mine. He teased me, nipping, licking, and tasting me until I was whimpering beneath him.

"I need you, Logan," I begged.

"I know. I need you, too," he agreed, pulling our bodies closer until I could feel them almost joined.

"I love you, Clare. My wife, my lover, my soul."

"I love you, too, Logan," I said and then two became one.

Our heated breaths and murmured words couldn't drown out the overwhelming emotions that hung in the air. Logan was mine and I was his. Forever.

His body owned mine, pushing it closer and closer to climax and I felt it in the pit of my belly like an inferno.

"That's it, Clare...let go," he said, and I did. I screamed out my pleasure at the same time he groaned out his own.

We spent the rest of our wedding night entwined

in each other, high on our love and intoxicated in the happiness of our marital bliss.

LOGAN

I awoke, bathed in ruby red curls and creamy soft skin. Clare's eyes were still closed and her breathing still even. She had an arm draped over my chest, and from this angle, I could see every glorious curve of her. I loved the way her waist curved in and flared out at her hip, and that perfect round ass she always complained about.

I didn't remember my life before her. I didn't want to. Every moment I'd spent before Clare and Maddie seemed like a blur; an endless blur of nothing to get me where I was today.

Laying in bed with my wife, with a daughter I couldn't wait to see, I now had a purpose. A calling in life.

I also had cancer.

Something that could tear me away from everything I held dear.

I would never tell her, but I was scared. Now that I had everything I'd ever wanted, I couldn't lose it. *I wouldn't.*

"Hey, you're awake," Clare said groggily.

I looked down on her sleepy face and smiled. "Yeah."

"What are you thinking about?" she asked.

"How beautiful you are," I lied.

"Hmm…I sure hope that's not what you were thinking about with that face. Try again."

This woman knew me inside and out. It was the reason she knew I was lying about leaving her the night I tried to walk away. She could see it in my eyes I didn't want to leave, and kept calling me out on my bullshit.

"You're scared," she said. It wasn't a question.

"Yes. A little," I admitted.

She lifted her head and rested her chin on my chest.

"I would be a little surprised if you weren't. Despite what Leah may think, you are not Superman."

"I know. I just want to be strong for you."

"And you are. You will be. But being scared of what might happen is normal, Logan."

I nodded and kissed her head.

"So, what do we do now?" I asked.

"We live our lives like we planned. We spend a week with our daughter." The fact that she just called Maddie "our daughter" made me instantly grin.

"We go home and we begin fighting. And we fight until we win. And we will win, Logan."

"And you're ready?" I asked, knowing everything she'd already gone through.

"I'm ready for anything, as long as you're there beside me, holding my hand."

"Forever," I vowed.

"Good," she grinned. "Well, Mr. Matthews, what do you want to do first?"

I paused for a moment, looking down at my naked wife. A million ideas came to mind, but there was only one that screaming at me.

"Honestly?" I asked.

"Of course."

"I want to go find our daughter and start living our life. I've never had a family and I'd really like to enjoy my new one."

She smiled, and lifted her head to kiss me, before pulling back.

"That is the best idea you've ever had. Let's go start our lives, Mr. Matthews."

And we did.

<hr>

Don't miss the next chapter of the Ready series. Leah and Declan's story continues in *Never Been Ready*.

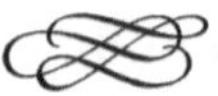

PROLOGUE

LEAH

I remember the shattering glass most of all. The sound still echoes through my head to this day. It was deafening to my child-sized eardrums, and I awoke quickly, covering my ears to try to mute the piercing sound.

The shrill voices came next. Heated, angry words were shouted outside my frilly pink bedroom that my mother and I had decorated from things we'd found at Goodwill. I was used to the shouting. My parents lived to fight. I spent a good part of my early childhood hidden behind the walls of that room. I'd play with my Barbies and dream of a normal family. Barbie would bake apple pie and sing Etta James in the kitchen, and Ken would take her out dancing. He would never raise his voice...or his hand. When I awoke that night though, it felt different...scarier. Even at seven, I knew something major was about to happen, and my world would never be the same.

Angry stomping passed my door, followed by hysterical cries and pleading words. Someone rushed down the hall, stopping briefly by my door, and then I heard the front door slam. Jumping out of my bed, I peeked my head out the door in the direction of our small living room. It was empty, and dark. The glass coffee table was in shards, and pieces were scattered all over the shaggy brown carpet. The dark shadows of the room seemed to be closing in on me from all angles. With the curiosity of a young child getting the best of me, I pressed on and walked farther into the room. No one was to be seen anywhere, and my exploration proved fruitless. Not knowing what else to do or where else to go, I picked a spot in the corner, curled myself into a ball, and started to count the glittery pieces of glass.

"What the hell are you doing out of bed?" my father asked when he found me some time later. My count had reached the hundreds by then, and my feet were ice cold from the lack of heat in the house. I looked up at the man I both loved and feared. Both of his hands were wrapped in bloody bandages and his clothes looked askew and out of place. I remember wondering if he had a hard time getting dressed with those bandages on his hands and that's why he looked so funny. I reminded myself to help Daddy button his shirt the next day. Children have such innocent minds.

"I couldn't sleep," I answered quietly, "Where's Mommy?"

"She's gone. For good."

CHAPTER ONE

LEAH

"How are you feeling, sweetie?" I asked the soon-to-be-mother as I walked into the birthing room carrying her chart and a cup of ice chips.

"I'm okay," she groaned before grimacing in pain as another contraction rolled through her tiny body.

Natural childbirth —I would never understand it. It was like going to the dentist and saying, "Novocain? No thanks. Just go in there Doc and rip that sucker right out!" Epidural was the way to go and it made my job so much easier.

I was a labor and delivery nurse and my current mother-to-be was named Hillary. With her granola eating boyfriend, Teegan, she had come in tonight with mild contractions after her water had broken. They were like any soon-to-be-parents —excited, nervous and scared. They were also very adamant in what they did and did not want. They had a three-page birthing plan. Three fucking pages that were single spaced no less. Hillary had promptly handed it to me in between her Lamaze breathing, and she'd instructed me to read and follow it to the letter.

Hippie chick was bossy. Five hours later, she was also bitch-ass tired and hadn't progressed at all. Stuck at six centimeters dilated, she was in a hell of a lot of pain and completely miserable.

Handing her the ice chips, I asked, "Can I get you anything?"

She shook her head and tried to give a polite smile, but I could see it waver. She was losing her strength fast. Hard lines from exertion showed in her forehead, sweat trickled down her brow and her eyes were heavy from exhaustion.

"Okay, I'll come back in a few and check on you." I gave a reassuring smile to Teegan before exiting the room.

Walking down the hall, I headed for the nurses station and spotted one of the other nurses on shift.

"Hey Trish. How's your night going?"

"Just finished delivering a baby boy. It was her third, so I think she could have done my job for me."

"I love the repeat offenders. They're so much easier."

"Yeah, but the newbies are fun too. Hey, I heard you went out with Susan's brother, Neil. How'd that go?" she asked, her eyes flickering with unshed laughter.

Neil and I had gone out the other night, and unfortunately it was three hours of my life I'd never get back. He was a financial advisor and he really loved his job. It had been all he talked about, and by the end of the evening —after repeated attempts at keeping myself from stabbing my own eyes out with a fork —I faked a stomachache and fled. It had been my first date in months —six months to be exact.

"Yes. Why do you say it like that? I asked, eyeing her suspiciously. "What do you know?"

"I'm surprised you made it out alive. Did he talk you to death? I thought I was going to bleed out from my ears from the endless chatter I had to endure on our date," she confessed.

"Oh my God! You went out with him, too? And you didn't feel the need to warn me? Shit, you could have told me he was a walking, talking, ad campaign for abstinence, " I scolded, causing her to burst into laughter.

She muffled the sound with her hand as a doctor walked by, and gave us a look that clearly held judgment, but I ignored it and pressed on.

"Seriously Trish! I thought you were my friend!"

"I'm sorry, Leah. I am. I didn't know. I found out afterwards, when Susan was talking about it in the cafeteria. She was so proud. She thought she'd finally found her new sister-in-law. Man, she is going to be disappointed."

"I have news for her. She's never, ever going to marry that man off. The only chance she has is finding a nice young girl who happens to be deaf."

We continued giggling and talking as I checked charts and entered a few things into the computer. When Susan asked if she could set me up with her hot brother, I leaped at the chance. My love life had taken a serious nose dive lately, and I was sick of sitting on the couch being utterly boring. I had no one to blame but myself. Well, that wasn't true. There was one other person I could blame for my complete lack of interest in the male species — Declan James.

Declan was childhood pals with my best friend's husband, Logan Matthews. Declan and I had met one night at a bar when Clare and Logan were dating. Declan had been an up-and-coming star in Hollywood, and well...he was gorgeous —like, sizzling hot, forgot-every-other-man-in-the-world-but-him-hot. Tall and rugged, with dark chocolate brown hair, he had hazel eyes that seemed to take on a life of their own, depending on his mood. Despite his obvious attempts to hide his appearance, I'd known who he was the minute he'd walked into that bar. Even with his dark sunglasses and baseball cap pulled tight against his head, I'd known.

I would recognize that weathered jawline and chiseled body anywhere. I'd spent enough hours looking at him on the internet, and even more time lying in bed, thinking of all the naughty things I could do to him if given the chance.

And suddenly there he had been, staring at me from across the bar. My wet dream had come to life. His eyes had locked with mine, making me feel hot and flustered. I didn't do flustered. Up until that point, I hadn't even been sure I'd understood the complete definition of the word.

I'd always been confident around men. They were fun and nice to be around, but some time ago, I'd come to the realization that they just weren't worth the trouble. I spent many good years of my adult life with one man who I thought was *the* man. When things got rough, he bailed. I was sick of investing my emotions and feelings into the part of our species who seemed unable to reciprocate. Men never followed through with their promise and they never loved me enough to stay. So, I'd sworn them off —until my eyes found Declan James, standing in a crowded bar, and I suddenly found myself unable to breathe.

By the time Logan and Declan had made it to our table that night, I had been nearly panting. My nether regions were on high alert, and wanted to play. I had to bite the inside of my cheek to keep from whimpering. By the time the two of us had been left alone, I had barely said two words to him. It hadn't been because I was star struck. The problem was I was so goddamn horny that my brain wouldn't function.

I kept telling myself, He's just another man...a really hot, yummy, lickable man. Stop drooling and say something.

But nothing had come out.

Eventually he'd spoken, and I had managed to get a few things out. What had I said? I had no fucking clue. I could have told him about puppies or the weather for all I knew. It was a wonder the man had wanted anything to do with me at all after that. But he had. We'd left together, and stopped at a local cemetery I'd apparently mentioned during our chat. He'd wanted to check it out before leaving town as a possible location for his upcoming film. It was a Civil War movie and Richmond, our home town, had been picked as one of the filming locations.

I'd watched him walk through the cemetery, looking at old graves and bending down to get different angles and views. His body had moved and flexed as he'd shifted positions, and I had to bite my lip to keep from groaning. I'd known him for all of two seconds, but I knew he was in his element in that cemetery.

After about fifteen minutes, I'd took him all in as he'd made his way back to where I had been standing, towards the entrance. His jeans had sat low on his hips and his black T-shirt accentuated the ridges of his abs. His eyes, no longer focused on the cemetery, had been dead set on me. He was male perfection.

"Looks good," he had announced, taking one final glance around. "I'll have the crew come out tomorrow during the day to take some photos that we can take back with us. But I think it's definitely a place we could use."

"This is your passion," I'd said softly.

He'd seemed a little taken aback by my sudden ability to form a coherent sentence, but he'd nodded, smiling.

"Yes. Acting is fun, but this is what I really want to do. Being behind the camera and creating something from start to finish is an amazing feeling."

It had been the first honest moment we had shared that evening. I finally hadn't felt flustered and it was the first time I noticed he wasn't paranoid about being recognized. He'd looked younger and more at ease. I'd smiled and relaxed a bit. I was still horny as hell, but calmer.

We'd eventually made it back to my townhouse where he'd showed me that all the ways he'd earned that bad-boy, lady-killer reputation he was known for. He'd ruined me for all other men that night.

For six months, I'd moped around, thinking about that night, unable to move on. I hadn't slept with another man, and every time I had gone to open my drawer full of stand-ins, the thought of using a vibrator had seemed less than thrilling when I knew what I was missing. The only times I'd managed to release some of the built-up steam had been when I thought of him. When I would touch myself, while remembering his hands touching me, and his lips tasting me, I could find bliss again. It was never as sweet, but it was as close as I'd ever get to him again. He was a player and I wasn't about to be his side dish. We had been doomed from the start.

I huffed out a sigh and said my good-byes to Trish before making my way back to the birthing room that held my New Age couple. Standing outside the room was Teegan. Bent forward, his hands were on his thighs, and his head was lowered. He looked ill. I knew this look well. It was the look of an expectant father about to lose his shit.

"Hey Teegan. How's it going?" I asked cautiously.

"It's...God, it's too fucking hard. She's in so much pain. I don't know what to do. I can't do this. I'm not ready." His breathing became labored as his head sank further between his knees.

"Teegan, look at me."

Nothing —he didn't budge.

"Teegan. It's time to man the fuck up. Look at me."

His eyes shot up to mine. That had gotten his attention. It usually did. I'd done this speech more than once.

"Hillary needs you right now. You need to get your shit together, go back in that room and take care of her. She doesn't have anyone else in there, except for you and me. As much as I want to help her, it's you she needs and loves. So, if you need to, give yourself a few more moments if you need them to breathe it out, but in a couple of minutes, you are going to walk back into that room and you will be the calm supportive man I know you can be. Got it?"

He looked at me. He was completely bewildered for a few seconds, but then he nodded and his lost vacant eyes changed. He became determined and full of driven purpose. I knew then that he was back where he needed to be.

We entered the room again together, and he immediately went to Hillary's side. He gave her a tender kiss on the forehead before he whispered something in her ear that made her smile.

It was a rough few more hours, but eventually

baby Kai entered the world. After cutting the umbilical cord, Teegan watched as I cleaned off his newborn son and then placed the baby into his arms.

I loved this part of my job. Humans were perfect in this moment. A new life was born, completely void of selfishness or sin. It was humanity at its best. When I saw a mother and father hold their child for the first time, I could see so many possibilities. A blank slate that could do and be anything, and I loved being the one to help usher him or her into the world.

"Thank you Leah," Teegan said, giving me a knowing smile.

"No problem pops. You did good."

"Do you have any children?" Hillary asked lovingly as she watched the two men in her life meet for the first time.

She smiled as Teegan carefully leaned down, nuzzling the three of them close together as a happy new family.

"No. No kids for me."

"Well there's still time. You will be a wonderful mother," Teegan said encouragingly.

I just smiled. There would be no children in my future. Children deserved to grow up in a loving home, with two parents who adored each other. I didn't have that. Besides, I had been raised in a house that was anything but loving. *What would I know about properly raising a child?*

The night air was chilly against my skin as I pulled my coat closer to my body. The thin scrubs that covered my legs were doing little to block the wind gusting through the parking lot of the hospital. Just as I reached my car, my purse started vibrating and playing the Superman theme song. I was a ringtone whore. I must have spent half my paycheck downloading songs and ringtones in iTunes store. I had a different ringtone for every person in my Contact List. I hand-selected the tone based on the person, making sure each song fit their personality. This particular ringtone, the one from the original movie, with its sweeping melodic ballad, was for Logan. He always reminded me of a super-hero because he was so giving and selfless, so I made him one —on my phone at least.

"Hey Superman. What's up?"

"Hey Leah. You still at work?"

"Well, technically, yes." I said, starting to do a little dance in the middle of the deserted parking lot in an effort to keep my toes from falling off.

"I'm in the parking lot. Why? Are you okay?"

Suddenly I was concerned. Logan had been diagnosed with Hodgkin's disease several months earlier, and although the prognosis looked good, after several rounds of chemotherapy and radiation, I still worried.

"Yeah, I'm fine. I'm actually here at work too."

Logan was a doctor and we worked at the same hospital. He worked in the emergency room though, so we very rarely saw each other.

"I wanted to ask a favor. We just had a pretty bad car accident come through. Trucker fell asleep at the wheel and veered off into oncoming traffic. Clipped a car, sending it head-on into a tree. We did everything we could for the driver, but she didn't make it. The trucker is fine, of course."

"What do you need me for Logan? You know I'm not trained in trauma, and it sounds like it's too late anyway."

"No, I know that." He paused as he let out a deep breath. "Leah, there's a kid."

I felt all the air leave my lungs at once. *Oh God, that poor child.*

"How old, Logan?"

"Seven."

"I'll be right there."

I walked back into the hospital, and headed towards the ER. Thoughts swarmed my mind as I tried to figure out what to do or say to a child who had just lost his mother. I was the same age when I'd lost mine. Granted, it wasn't the same situation. His hadn't chosen to leave him. But it was still a loss. I knew what it could do to a child. The loss could eat away, slowly taking that childhood innocence until there's nothing but bitterness and longing. If it hadn't been for my best friend Clare and her family, I would have been swallowed by it.

I rounded the corner and found Logan reviewing a file at the nurse's station. He looked tired and worn. We'd tried to talk him into taking time off, but he'd refused. He'd said he would go fucking nuts if he was left with nothing to do. We had managed to get him to reduce his hours and work part-time during his treatments, but on nights like this, when the job got rough, I could see it wearing on him.

"Hey, how are you doing?" I asked.

He looked up at me and at that moment, I knew what losing a patient meant to him. He was destroyed.

"Oh God, Logan...I'm sorry," I said, pulling him into a tight hug.

I'd lost patients before. I knew the pain and guilt, worrying that I could have done more. I remembered the few I'd lost like it was yesterday. I remembered their names, the parents who grieved the lost lives and the years that had passed by without them.

"I don't know why this one is affecting me so

much more. It's not like this is the first time I've lost someone on the table."

"You're a father now Logan." I said, pulling back from our embrace.

"Every mother you save is Clare. Every child you bandage up is Maddie. It's harder now to separate yourself from your patients because *you* feel so much more."

"You're right. I can't stop thinking about that child. He's parentless now. There is no father on record and the police can't find a next of kin. He told the officers at the scene they were on their way to visit a close family friend so I guess they're trying to make contact with them. Social services is on their way."

"Hey, it's okay. You did everything you could. Go home. Be with your wife and daughter and let them help you get through this. I've got this. I'll take care of him until Social Services come, all right?"

He nodded before pulling me into another hug.

We said our good-byes, and I made my way towards the room that held the child. His name was Connor. He sustained only mild injuries from the accident, since he'd been in the back of the car.

Right before I was about to push open the door open, I paused, feeling panic rise in my chest.

What was I doing?

I should find someone else to go in there —a

mother maybe, someone who would know what to say or do. I didn't have any experience with children beyond my goddaughter, Maddie. What the hell did I know about caring for a hopeless child? Isn't that something I should have learned from my own parents? All I learned from my mother and father was how to abandon and hurt.

Looking around the empty hallway, I realized there was no one else. It was only me. I had to do something. I entered the room, and my heart fell. He was sitting in the center of the bed with knees pulled to the center of his chest and his head lowered. He was clutching something in his left hand, but I couldn't make out what it was. *A paper, or a photo maybe?* Tears trickled down his legs, and I heard him heave in a breath as he sobbed.

As I clicked the door shut, his eyes jerked up and found me. They were hazel and looked like paint splatters. Blue, green, and brown were mixed together to create one of the most beautiful sets of eyes I'd ever seen. They were so unique, yet familiar. I felt the overwhelming need to pull him into my arms and tell him everything would be okay even though I had no proof otherwise.

"Who are you?" he questioned.

"I'm Leah."

"Are you here to take me away?" he asked cautiously.

"No, I'm not taking you anywhere. I'm a nurse."

"They already put bandages on me."

"I know," I said.

"So, why are you here?" he asked softly. He quickly wiped away the tears from his eyes in a half-hearted effort to cover up the fact that he'd been crying.

"I'm here so you don't have to be alone. You can talk to me if you want, or you can ignore me, but I'm going to sit here with you until it's time to leave because I think you need a friend right now."

"You're not my friend," he retorted.

"No, but I'd like to be."

BUY NOW

ACKNOWLEDGMENTS

Since this is a novella and this things are supposed to be short and sweet, I'm going to continue that theme through to the very end—including the acknowledgments.

Next month, I will be celebrating my one year anniversary of becoming a published author. Since that infamous night not too long ago that I hit publish on Amazon and my world literally exploded, I have been amazed by the generosity and compassion of those I've met along the way. I have made life long friends and formed connections with people all over the world, and I know I say this all the time, but I really do have the best readers ever.

Thank you to each and every one of you who has made this crazy dream of mine a reality. I love you all!

J.L. Berg is the USA Today bestselling author of the Ready Series, the Lost & Found series, and many more. Originally from California, she now resides in central Virginia with her high school sweetheart, two children, and three dogs. When she's not writing, she enjoys spending time with her family or indulging in her love for Doctor Who. J.L. Berg is represented by Jill Marsal of Marsal Lyon Literary Agency, LLC. For the latest book updates, audio news, and more, be sure to visit her website.

www.ingramcontent.com/pod-product-compliance
Lightning Source LLC
Chambersburg PA
CBHW061545310726
48972CB00008B/2617